STAR SPLIT

KATHRYN LASKY

Hyperion Books for Children
New York

The fragment from the poem "In the Silver" by Jennifer Clement is taken from the book
The Tree Is Older Than You Are (Simon & Schuster, New York City) and *Newton's Sailor*
(Ediciones El Tucan de Virginia, Mexico) and is printed with the author's permission.

For information address Hyperion Books for Children, 114 Fifth Avenue, New York,
New York 10011-5690.
First Edition
1 3 5 7 9 10 8 6 4 2
Printed in the United States of America.
Library of Congress Cataloging-in-Publication Data
Lasky, Kathryn.
Star split/Kathryn Lasky.—1st ed.
p.   cm.
Summary: In 3038, thirteen-year-old Darci uncovers an underground movement to save
the human race from genetic enhancement technology.
ISBN 0-7868-0459-9 (trade: alk. paper)—ISBN 0-7868-2401-8 (lib.: alk. paper)
[1. Genetic engineering—Fiction. 2. Cloning—Fiction. 3. Science fiction.] I. Title
PZ7.L3274St 1999
[Fic]—dc21 98-43839

For Max and Meribah,
who make me believe in the future

An Old Night

WHEN THE NIGHT GREW THIN THAT is when the dream would come, on the frayed blackness before the dawn. . . .

Sudden white light. Blinding white light splintering the darkness of her sleep. Darci was blinking. But how can you blink in a dream? Her eyes were already closed. This was a dream, wasn't it? And sleep is dark not white light. She must get through this hot whiteness. She would try creeping to the edge—what edge? Where was she? But she had to get to the edge because that's where she would find a shadow to crouch in. But what edge? A force drove her back from it but another dared her . . . another. There was another. She was sure of that.

"Another what?"

"Just another. Don't ask. Go to the edge."

"Go to the edge of what?"

Darci awoke with a jolt. She blinked. The blackness of the night was beginning to fade to gray. She was shaking. Her nightgown stuck to her sweaty body. The dream was too real. She felt too close to some terrible edge. She clutched her pillow and looked out the window. One star still hung in the sky. She was confused. Was it the first star of the night or the last one of the morning? Her body was trembling. She was used to rock edges but this was no rock edge—it was like the edge of the sky. Could one fall off the edge of the sky, tumble from the rim of a universe? She closed her eyes now to erase the night and the white light came back like splinters beneath her eyelids.

When she woke in the morning Darci Murlowe remembered hardly anything except a star. A star and a single word, "another." That was all. Yet she had dreamed the dream for months now, maybe her entire lifetime, for it seemed as if this dream had crouched somewhere in the gray shadows of her mind forever, just waiting.

Chapter 1

THE MURLOWES GATHERED AROUND the television in their living room. Although the program would not start for a few minutes, Darci's parents and grandparents spoke in hushed voices. They did not want to miss one second, not one breath, not one syllable of the annual Reading of the Lists. It was the most important event of the entire year in the Bio Union.

Darci was thirteen. She had not been allowed to watch until she was nine, and then her parents, who were usually not strict or rule-prone, had told her exactly what kind of behavior they expected. Absolutely no talking, no fidgeting, no shifting seats, no eating.

Darci had found it immensely boring that first year,

but now she understood it better. Its meaning. She knew which names her parents were listening for and on the rare occasions when one was read she could see them squeeze each other's hands in a silent kind of ecstasy. Her grandparents reacted similarly. It was more exciting of course if you were a grown-up, for there was always a chance that there might be the name of someone you knew. There was never the chance of a child's name appearing on the list of New Endowments.

The first strains of the anthem sounded. The silence in the living room deepened, becoming a palpable thing in itself. Her grandfather leaned forward a bit.

The announcer's voice filled the living room: "Ladies and gentlemen, the Prima of the Bio Union."

Darci was always struck by how small the Prima appeared when she was behind the podium. Her blonde hair glistened sleek and shining like the helmet of a warrior from ancient times. Her lovely sea green eyes blinked once, twice, and then she began to speak. "Good People, it is with immense pride that in the year 3038, the tenth year of my Primarchy, I again have the privilege of announcing the names of the men and women nominated by the Board of Selection for Endowment through Umbellation.

"As you know, to be selected for umbellation is the highest accolade our Union can confer on any individual. For those children who are listening . . ."

Every year the Prima said the same thing: that genes were not everything; that just because we lived in an era of the most advanced technologies for reproductive genetics it did not guarantee that one would become an Endowment Laureate. These people whose names would be read tonight had indeed gone beyond the most optimistic predictions of their genotype; and for this reason these individuals had been selected.

The camera came in close for now she would begin the Reading of the Lists. It was from these humans that cells would be collected and placed in the cryogenic repositories at The Sanctum of Bestowal in the capital city. And it was from these cells that umbulae would be created.

The Prima herself was an umbula. Nearly one thousand years ago, the first Prima had given cells from a single scraping on the interior of her mouth and now thirty-two generations later this Prima, the thirty-second copy of the first, began speaking the names—the names for immortality.

Chapter 2

Darci squeezed her eyes shut as the champagne cork popped.

"To Edmar Golenc." Her father's voice seemed as bubbly as the champagne.

"I can't believe it! I just can't believe it," her grandmother kept saying over and over while shaking her head. "Oh, Rufus!" She turned to Darci's grandfather. "Did you ever think we would live to see this day—a Zolnotz selected for Endowment? A Zolnotz, Rufus! What would your father have said?"

"I think"—Darci's grandfather ran his fingers through the nimbus of silver hair that encircled his bald dome—"I think that the man many recognized as one of the greatest language scientists of the Bio Union would have been speechless!" Everyone laughed at this. "Leon, pour a little champagne for Darci. She can have a sip."

"What will the kids in school say tomorrow?" asked her grandmother. "There are quite a few Zolnotz in your class, aren't there?" Darci nodded. The fizz from the champagne tickled the underside of her nose. She was really not thinking about the Zolnotz kids or the others in her school. She was suddenly caught by a strange thought. What did the Originals do on this night, the Reading of the Lists? It was after all almost like a holiday, for it celebrated the cornerstone of the Reproductive Reformation and the Bio Union—umbellation. And although few were umbellated, the Originals did not even have a hope of achieving such an honor. They could only afford to reap the most basic benefits from genetic enhancement—the fundamental health guarantees against crippling genetic illnesses and diseases. It was as if the whole Bio Union was having a party and the Originals couldn't even come, or at best they had to sit apart at a kind of "children's table." Darci always hated when people invited her family to a big party and then the children were seated separately. There was something very insulting about being physically placed apart, even if you were the kind of person who, like Darci, sometimes did feel somewhat separate from people. She could live with feeling apart or slightly different, but on her terms, not those defined by others. Now on this night she just bet that Originals felt very apart, and not on their own terms at all but those specified by the Bio Union.

The more she thought about it the more disturbed she became. Before she realized it she had blurted out the question. There was a sudden silence, then nervous laughter. Darci's mother, Juditha, blushed a deep rosy color until her face nearly matched her red hair. "Darci! You come up with the oddest questions!"

"I'm sure I don't know," Darci's grandmother said, and nervously adjusted her bun. "But I don't think you should trouble yourself with the thought, dear."

Darci was embarrassed too. She supposed that it was wrong at a time of celebration, especially this of all years when for the first time ever a Zolnotz was being endowed. How could she think about Originals? She looked down into her glass and stuck just the tip of her tongue into the champagne. She liked the feel of the champagne on her tongue more than the actual taste.

The conversation soon got on track again.

"Venka, what do you mean, will you be invited to the Endowment Procedure?" Darci's mother said. "Of course you will be. I am sure that The Academy is just now making a list of every prominent Zolnotz in the Bio Union. You think that the first Zolnotz ever umbellated is not going be made a big deal of? I mean, this is basic public relations."

"But Leon was his student." Venka nodded at her son, Darci's dad. "And you because you're married to Leon and have designed computer programs for Edmar, you'll be invited. But really I don't know why Rufus and myself . . ."

"Quit worrying, woman!" Darci's grandfather said. "Edmar and I knew each other at the Institute. Our fathers were friends. Our mothers, I think, played cards together."

Darci had decided long ago that her grandmother's perpetual state of mind was one of worrying. She had a career in the arts and had been an outstanding track star in her day, but she had married into a family of scientists. She always thought of herself as a sort of odd person out. But she wasn't. She was just what the Murlowes needed in terms of their family gen pro, genetic profile. As her husband often said, she was "a jock and an artist."

"I think Darci will be invited too," Juditha added.

"Mom, you're kidding. What will I wear? Can I get a new dress? I hated that dress I had to wear in Elise's wedding. I looked so stupid."

"You looked adorable!" her grandmother said.

"Navy blue is not my color. I am too washed out for navy blue."

"It wasn't navy blue. It was sapphire," her mother said.

"That's just the point. On me sapphire turns to just plain dark blue!"

"No, not at all!" Her dad came over and gave her a squeeze." But I do think that this is an occasion deserving of a new dress."

"Yeah! I saw this great dress in *Now*."

"What's *Now*?" her dad asked.

"It's the fashion magazine you and Mom gave me for my last birthday, puleeze! Anyway. It was this really pretty pink mesh material."

"Mesh!" Venka squeaked. "You'll be naked. Mesh is see-through."

"No, Grandma. There's an underdress, and then appliquéd on top of the mesh are flowers. Oh, it's so pretty."

"It sounds kind of dressy," said Juditha. "I think the ceremony is usually a daytime event. More tailored. If it is evening and black tie for men then that would be more appropriate. I'm sure we can find you a nice suit for daytime."

"A suit! Mom, I'm a kid."

"Maybe we can all have a grand shopping expedition and get us all fitted out!" Venka said.

Oh, great! thought Darci, just what she always dreamed of: clothes shopping with her mom and grandmother. Their taste was so . . . so, oh gosh, it was so *third millennium* for lack of a better term.

Chapter 3

AFTER HER GRANDPARENTS HAD departed Darci went upstairs to bed. She heard her parents downstairs still talking about their mentor and teacher, Edmar Golenc. Her mother was going to call a florist first thing in the morning and send a bouquet of Edmar's favorites, lilies, to his office.

As Darci washed her face for bed she studied it carefully for any signs of zits. For Otherness sake! She hoped she didn't get zits like her friend Pearl. One thousand years of genetic enhancement technology and still there were zits! It didn't seem fair. It wasn't fair. They could have gotten rid of zits. Zits were a no-brainer compared to the other things the reprogeneticists had conquered—

cystic fibrosis, Down's syndrome, cancer. But it had been the decision of the Congress in the previous millennium, which was responsible for setting up the Board of Selection, that only the most life-threatening diseases would be eliminated through genetic enhancement therapy. It was in fact against the law and the Statutes of Trait Selection to select for beauty, skin color, hair types—including the trait for baldness, which her grandfather shared—any of the traits that were termed "the Vanities" or "the Vanity Genes." So there were still people walking about with noses that they considered too long or too broad, eyes that were too close together, hair too frizzy or straight, and worst of all, zits! One would have thought that none of those people in that Congress or on the Board of Selection had ever been teenagers.

Darci studied her face again. She wondered if she did get zits if her freckles would perhaps camouflage them. She didn't have that many, but in the summertime they sprung up in a distinctive band that stretched across her nose and then ran up toward her cheekbones. She didn't mind them really. In full summer the clusters of freckles swirled on her cheekbones like spiral galaxies. She had the complexion of a redhead like her mother, but her hair was jet-black and curly—a mass of cowlicks that whirled around her head in an unmanageable fury, forcing her to keep her hair short. She did have her mother's eyes, however. They were eyes that seemed to change color depending on the light. Sometimes they were clear green, sometimes hazel flecked with gold, and sometimes what she thought of as a glacial green, with a hint of blue way, way down, like the waters of a glacial lake. Darci took a cotton square and mopped a stingy liquid across her face. Well, one couldn't have everything, she guessed. And once more she suddenly thought of the Originals.

It was not as if the Originals didn't have anything. They were in many instances extraordinarily beautiful. Still, they could also have zits. But what they did not have was the extra pair of chromosomes, or what was now called the forty-eighth chromosome. With this extra unit more genetic material could be installed. The forty-eighth chromosome was the invention of Madeline Gaston several centuries before. She had been umbellated, and Darci's own father had studied under a third-generation umbula of the first Madeline.

Every human born within the last one thousand years had benefited to some degree from genetic enhancement. Basic embryo diagnosis was available for everyone no matter how rich or how poor. If a defective gene was detected, one that would cause leukemia or cystic fibrosis or some dread disease or disability, it could be eliminated through embryonic inoculation, which in essence corrected the defective gene. However, it cost money to go beyond these basic health services. The richer, the more educated, were of course able to acquire the forty-eighth chromosome. And only one generation had to acquire it for it to be passed down. Darci's ancestors on her mother's and father's sides, going back for centuries to the very dawn of genetic enhancement and umbellation, had been in such a favored position.

People who possessed this extra set of chromosomes were known as Genhants, or Genetically Enhanced Humans. They had passed their amazingly rich legacy with the forty-eighth chromosome down through generations. Thus Darci was a Genhant. She went to a Genhant school and Genhant summer camps. The art classes she took outside of school were usually filled with Genhants, although sometimes there was an Original who had received a scholarship.

Darci got along fine with them. She didn't find them that different. Oh, their grammar might not be quite as good, but especially in art they seemed to Darci just as capable. There was one boy, an Original, in her Arts in the City class during spring break last year who came up with the most amazingly detailed drawings. And his sense of color was extraordinary.

Darci now crawled into bed still thinking about Genhants and Originals. As was so often true if you just began to think about the words themselves, they started to sound funny. Genhant, she understood. There was a logic to it. But what did the word "original" really mean? How had they come up with that word for these nongenetically enhanced humans? Why had they not called them Non-Gens instead of Originals? It would have seemed more logical. She supposed it was rather negative to call someone a "Non" anything. Darci often thought about words and their meanings. She came by it naturally. After all, her great-grandfather had been a language scientist. He might have known something about the word "original." Sometimes words, or rather the names of things, sounded so arbitrary, so irrational, as if a bunch of letters had just been flung together on a whim. Why, for example, was a daisy called a daisy?

Now Darci's mind turned to the pink mesh dress with the appliquéd flowers. She hoped the ceremony was an evening event. Black tie. She yawned and laughed. Black tie and pink mesh with daisies—and were there lilies too? Edmar Golenc's favorite. She was on that fuzzy border of wake and sleep, but what did the word "original" mean, exactly? Where had it come from?

Chapter 4

"Mom," Darci said as she flexed her foot and stretched the large elastic band anchored to one leg of the kitchen table.

"I wish you would do those exercises elsewhere. Mornings are confusing enough around here." Juditha Murlowe was racing around the kitchen making breakfast as well as trying to pack Darci's lunch for school. She was always a bit frazzled in the morning, especially Tuesday mornings when she liked to get to BOG early, for she had a full three hours guaranteed on Herman, the mega computer.

"This table is the only place I can attach the theraband and get the right angle." Darci never missed doing her flexing exercises. When she was just an infant she had been stricken by the terrible airborne virus, a mutated form of a stronichylimia, a disease that had raged more than a thousand years before in the twentieth century. Many infants had died, others were left with permanent muscular weakness and even paralysis. Darci's right foot and ankle had been affected. Indeed, her right foot was a size and a half smaller than her left. She had had to wear a brace until she was four. But she was so diligent about her exercises that she had regained full strength. Except for the size difference, the orthopedic surgeon said the feet were identical in terms of their muscle tone and strength. Darci's grandmother had been a track champion, but Darci had found that her feet, her legs, just wanted to climb more than run. She had loved rock climbing since the very first time she had ever seen a television program about it.

At her school there was a rock-climbing club and Darci was secretary/treasurer of it. They went on expeditions and she was responsible for running the bake sales and other projects that raised money for them. This summer she would be allowed to go away to rock-climbing camp. Finally! Everyone else in the club had been going for at least two years. But Juditha and Leon Murlowe felt that she was too young. That was Darci's only real gripe about her parents. They clung. Clung like crazy. When the other kids were allowed to stay for all-day preschool, Darci's mother, still working only half-time, would pick her up every day after lunch. She would have given anything to stay for the whole day. They got to do such great things. Field trips. A magician once came and taught every kid a trick. The next day Darci was the only one who couldn't do a trick. It was so humiliating.

She looked down at her foot now—forty more reps. She could eat and do the exercises at the same time.

"So what were you about to ask me?" Her mom plopped down across from her with the special edition of the newspaper. But she wasn't really listening, Darci could tell. And then, as if to confirm this, her mother broke in and began reading from the newspaper. "If you know anything about a particular subject it can be really disturbing to read about it in the newspaper. The media always can screw something up just a little bit. Listen to this: 'Edmar Golenc, reprogeneticist, pioneered laser penetration and surgical techniques used on the twenty-second chromosome and the pair bases of adenine. His work ultimately was responsible for the eradication of several immunodeficient diseases that began to be expressed in the last three decades.'"

"So what's the big deal?" Darci asked, looking up from her cereal.

"It wasn't adenine bases he worked with. It was the guanine. And it was only because of his work on the twenty-*first* chromosome that he was able to develop these techniques in the first place. I mean, they really should get the story straight here."

Darci shrugged. It didn't seem like a big deal to her, but her parents, both having spent their careers at the Board of Genetic Engineering, or BOG, got a little excited about such things. "I'm going to talk to Suzy Purcell about this."

"Who's Suzy Purcell?"

"Press officer for BOG." Juditha looked up from the paper. "Now, what was your question?"

"My question?" Darci had almost forgotten. She looked blank for a moment "Oh yeah, I remember. Mom, what does the word 'original' mean?"

"Well, Darci, you know that. It means that unfortunately these people do not have the forty-eighth chromosome. For one reason or another they couldn't afford to get one, or in most cases their ancestors couldn't. They're not genetically enhanced as we are. But now actually there's talk of some government assistance to allow that in certain cases."

"No, that's not what I'm talking about. I mean what does the word itself mean? How did they ever dream that word up for them? Why didn't they call them something else?"

Juditha looked at her daughter as if completely bewildered. "Like what?"

"I don't know . . . like Googlefoons."

"Googlefoons? What are Googlefoons?"

"I don't know, I just made it up. Strung together a bunch of funny sounds and syllables, I guess."

"Original?" Juditha said the word softly. "It is sort of a funny-sounding word when you think about it. I'm sure your great-grandfather would have known. He was on the Naming Committee for new technologies, professor of genetic linguistics. Thought up a lot of those names for many of the procedures we use at BOG, but I don't have the slightest idea where that word 'original' came from. I guess if you really wanted to explore it you should write to the Palmyra Institute where your grandfather taught, contact someone at the Library of Dead Language. There are verbal paleontologists at the library trained by your great-grandfather. They are pretty old themselves now. You know, it might make an interesting project. Don't you have to do a big research composition in the spring?"

Darci tried not to groan. This was the other not-so-great thing about her mom. Juditha Murlowe saw an educational project in everything. She was a constant source of suggestions for school projects, science fair experiments, essays, things to do for extra credit. "You want me to have my secretary call up there and see who you might speak to?"

"No, Mom! No. I was just wondering, that's all."

"Well, it's a very interesting question." Juditha began to gather up her briefcase. "Original." She said the word again softly, then came over and kissed Darci on the cheek. "Have a nice day at school, sweetie."

"Have a nice day at BOG."

"Love you!" Juditha did her little wink and funny wave as she went out the kitchen door to her car.

"Love you too, Mom," Darci said. But apparently not loudly enough. In a split second Juditha's dainty face peeked around the door again. "I said, 'Love you too, Mom.'"

"Gosh, I hope I'm not going deaf. It's nowhere in our gen pro."

"You probably have wax in your ears, Mom."

"You're right, sweetie. Love you again."

"Love you again!" This time Darci said it loud and clear.

And she meant it. She loved her mom. Her quirky, bubbly, slightly driven mom.

Chapter 5

"I'M TELLING YOU THE TRUTH!" MARILYN Hammertz was lifting her right hand as if she were about to testify in a court of law. "If my grandfather were alive today he would have been the first Zolnotz to be umbellated. He did all that work on the nineteenth chromosome. Not only that, he was an outstanding lawyer who revised the Statutes of Trait Selection for the new millennium. A reprogeneticist, a Supreme Court Justice . . ."

But it wasn't a court of law. It was the school yard. Darci hated Marilyn Hammertz. She was obnoxious, stuck up, and thought she knew everything. "We were at a party last night for the Reading of the Lists and everyone said as soon as Edmar Golenc's name was read, 'It should have been Rudy Hammertz!' I'm telling you the truth."

"Well, I'm telling you the truth, Marilyn. He ain't alive, sweetheart! And half of life is showing up, as they say." Darci thrilled as Max Lasovetch spat out the words.

There was no one quite like Max. He was often surly, sometimes considered a discipline problem, a definite underachiever who had already been thrown out of two schools. "Three and you're out, Max," the principal had said, which meant the next school he would go to would be one for Originals. But people basically liked Max despite his snarling and stubborn ways. Darci had a feeling they would never throw him out. He made life interesting. And sometimes, rarely in the classroom, Max Lasovetch was brilliant, like now.

"So we don't need to be hearing about your grandfather," Max continued. "It wasn't his fault that he wasn't selected for endowment, but it seems really rude and ungracious of you to stand out here and take away from Edmar Golenc's moment."

"It's not just a moment, Max. It's forever. Umbellation is forever, you dolt." Marilyn began to speak in a breathy dramatic tone that Darci thought was so fake. "We have lost my grandfather forever!"

"I know it's forever, and bad manners are only for the moment." Max spoke with a sly arrogance that made the others laugh softly. "Look, a lot of our parents were taught by Golenc and I just think it is extremely offensive to hear you speak this way. So just live with it, Marilyn!"

"SB!" she spat.

Another expression that had become totally meaningless, Darci thought. Who knew what those two letters meant now? You just said it when you wanted to insult the content of what someone had said, not necessarily the person.

Marilyn turned and walked away in a huff. Her gang, many of the most popular kids in the school, followed. But one or two looked back at Max with what Darci felt was wonder bordering on longing.

The other kids had straggled into school for the starting bell after lunch, but Darci lagged behind.

"Max?" Darci said.

"Yeah?"

"You know that thing you said."

"What thing?"

"The thing about half of life is showing up . . . you said someone once said it. Who?"

"Oh, I'm not sure. It was a fragment on a compressed vis-aud disk from over a thousand years ago. My older brother works on restoration of those."

"Where's that?"

"Palmyra."

"The Library of Dead Language?"

"Yeah, the lab's a part of that. In the summer I usually go and stay with him for a month. I might even get an internship this summer. Unpaid, of course. There's a rock-climbing camp near there, up at Arc of the Winds in the Kerals."

"You're kidding!" Darci exclaimed.

"No. Lots of the guys at the lab rock climb. Not me. I try to exert myself as little as possible." Max said this with a completely straight face.

"Oh, gee, I've got to go there. You know, my great-grandfather was a language scientist at the Library of Dead Language."

"And needless to say should have been the first Zolnotz umbellated."

"Of course!" Darci laughed. "That's what all our friends say, and our relatives." She imitated Marilyn's breathy voice.

"Yeah, mine too."

"Hey, I just thought of something else. Maybe you know this from the Dead Language lab."

"What's that?"

"Well, first of all what does 'SB' mean?"

"Oh, that's easy. Shitbull."

"What does it mean, though?"

"Comes from two words actually—shit which is like, you know, excrement, waste, bowel stuff. And bull, bull is an extinct animal."

"Why would that be so insulting? I mean what's wrong with excrement? It fuels everything now."

"I know, but you have to figure way back when it could have meant something else. Maybe it wasn't so useful. Maybe it was another color, not so fragrant, and who knows what kind of an animal a bull really was—maybe really dumb."

"Yeah. I guess so. Okay, here's another one for you."

"What's that?"

"Original—what does the word really mean?"

"Oh, gee, I have no idea. I know what you mean, though. The word doesn't seem to have any logic to it at all. That's a problem for the lab's top language scientists." Darci began to head back into school. "Wanna cut?"

"Cut?"

"Yeah. What's your next period?"

"Gym."

"Mine too. I make it a practice to cut gym at least once a month." Darci looked at Max. He was a curious one. "Come on."

Darci had never cut a class in her life. "Where do you go when you cut?"

"Malben's."

"You're kidding." Malben's was a hangout for Originals. It was right across the street from their high school. "Okay," Darci said suddenly. She was a bit surprised with the quickness of her reply. She followed Max off the school grounds.

"They have something called a liquid sundae here that is really great. Cherry is the best flavor," Max said as they slid into a booth. "Want one?"

"Sure." Darci replied.

"Two liquid cherries," Max called to the man behind the counter.

Just then a group of kids walked in. Darci craned her neck around the edge of the booth for a better glimpse.

"Don't stare too hard, Darci. This is their ground. They're going to know we're Genhants, so just try to kind of blend in."

At that moment a girl swept by their booth. She knocked Darci's sweater to the floor by accident.

"Oh! Sorry, dishy."

The word fell on Darci's ears, exotic and dangerous. It was a word Originals used all the time. She wasn't sure what it meant. It was generally positive, but there was something edgy, risky about it. The girl bent over to pick up Darci's sweater. Their eyes met. The girl was startlingly beautiful. Her skin tone was a deep reddish-brown, almost like amber. Her eyes blue-gray with long lashes that curled back. Her hair was dark brown with glints of gold. A sudden coldness crept into the girl's eyes as they met Darci's. She snorted and shoved the sweater into Darci's hands. Darci knew instantly what the girl was thinking: why had she wasted a word like "dishy" on a Genhant? The girl was embarrassed. Max looked down and studied the table hard as if it were the most intriguing thing in the world. Darci looked down immediately. There was an unwritten code that when one might have disturbed an Original in any way one avoided eye contact. It was one's duty to appear submissive. This usually seemed to have a calming effect. The girl swaggered off.

Max got up to get their liquid sundaes. Darci had kept her eyes down but now stole a glance to the other end of the room where the group of Originals sat at the counter. They were quiet, but there seemed to be a lot of communication on a nonverbal level transpiring between them. It was known that Originals were generally not a talkative lot, especially when they were out in public. But they did use their hands and flick their heads in a unique manner. Darci heard the word "dishy" again several more times. No wonder Max liked to come here. It was fascinating to watch them in a group. If it had been a group of Genhant teenagers it would have been a totally different feeling. There would have been much more noise for one thing. Loud talk, laughter. Maybe some jumping around, playful physical contact. But these kids were different. They came with a quietness, and their movements were fluid and graceful with subtle shadows of meaning. Their eyes seemed incredibly expressive, as if they had a language all their own. But Darci could not watch their eyes that much for it would certainly attract their attention and this was the last thing she wanted to do.

Max sipped his liquid sundae. "They're different, aren't they?" He spoke softly. "You never notice that much until they are in a group. It's the way they communicate with one another. Their gestures."

"Yeah, and their eyes."

"Whatever you do, don't focus on their eyes."

"I won't. You come here a lot?"

"Yeah."

Darci didn't have to ask him why. It was something she felt too. Something inexpressible. There was the feeling of danger, but another thing beyond that. There was a sense of rareness and somehow freshness about these young Originals. Their very presence was invigorating.

"They don't mind us as long as we just keep our eyes down and don't use our loud Genhant talk."

So that was exactly what Darci and Max did. Kept their eyes down, spoke in whispers, and sipped their liquid cherry sundaes until it was time for them to go back to school for the last two periods of the day.

Chapter 6

"Mom! Mom!" Darci heard the front gate swing shut and before her mother could get to the door Darci was halfway down the walk waving a colorful flyer in her hand. "Mom, this is so great, like the greatest camp, you've got to let me go. Oh, please, Mom, I'll do anything. I'll get a baby-sitting job and help pay for it. I'll give up my allowance until summer. Please let me go!"

"Hang on, Darci, let me get the groceries inside."

"I'll cook dinner. I'll clean up the kitchen every night. I'll . . . I'll . . ." Darci had run out of parent-pleasing propositions.

"Now, what is this all about?" Juditha said, sinking

down into a kitchen chair. Darci had already begun to unpack the groceries.

"Oh, Mom, it's so great. You and Dad have just got to let me go. First Max Lasovetch told me about it, and then I went to the resource teacher and she gave me all these pamphlets. This is just its second year. That's why I hadn't heard of it. But she said and our rock-climbing club advisor said that it was the best rock-climbing camp in the Bio Union. It's called Arc of the Winds."

"Arc of the Winds—that's where the Prima's summer palace is."

"I know that's where it is. It's those same mountains—the Kerals. Actually it's not that far from the Palmyra Institute. See, I could climb and do research at the Library of Dead Language. It could be a true growth experience—intellectually and physically, Mom."

Juditha Murlowe smiled. "You know how to appeal, don't you, sweetie? Mind, body. But Palmyra and this Arc of the Winds place is very far. It'll be expensive getting there."

Darci whipped out the second brochure. "I know, but guess what. They have special student rates, or camper rates. Look, Mom, it's no more than going to that stupid crafts camp that Pearl went to last year and hated. Her parents thought there was a very bad element of Originals there. Too many scholarships."

"So the bad news," Juditha said, studying the

brochures, "with this place is that there are no scholarships, but the good news is that there is not the 'bad element' of Originals." A slight bitterness had crept into
Juditha's voice, and Darci noticed the corners of her
mom's mouth curl into sourish lines, as if she had tasted
something bad. Darci wasn't quite sure what to make of
her mom's reaction. It seemed odd. She had expected
her to complain about the expense and the distance, but
her mom almost seemed angry. Darci had this sad sinking feeling in her chest. Her mom looked up. Her expression softened.

"You really want to go, don't you, baby?" Darci
squeezed her eyes shut. This was just the problem. Her
mom wanted to keep her a baby. It wasn't right. It was
really both their problem and Darci didn't know how to
solve it.

"Mom, you've got to let me go. I mean, you've just
got to." Darci blinked, startled by her own words. Her
mother appeared startled too. Juditha reached for
Darci's hand and squeezed it. "You're right. I know it."

Darci felt a glimmer of hope. "Mom, it's going to be
fine. Hundreds and thousands of kids go to camps,
sleepover camps for the summer. This camp has the
highest rating in terms of safety and level of climbing
expertise of the staff. Mom, I have only, for the most
part, climbed in gyms, on Teflex walls. Except for that
day camp last year where they only took us to those

rocks right outside of town. Grandma could have walked over those rocks. Even our instructors say that climbing in gyms can't teach you everything you need to know about safe climbing. It's never the same as outdoors. There's no wind, for one thing."

Juditha sighed. *Please don't say we'll think about it,* Darci prayed. That was always a bad sign. "Okay," her mother said in a steady voice. "We'll talk with Dad about it tonight. I think your grandparents might be happy to contribute something toward the cost."

"Oh, Mom!" Darci jumped up. Even though her mother was two or three inches taller, Darci picked her up a few inches off the floor and scuttled about the kitchen carrying her. "You're the greatest. Oh, Mom!" she squealed. "I'm sure they have a visiting weekend. You and Dad can come, and Grandma and Grandpa."

"That really *would* cost money!"

Finally Darci set her mother down. "Oh, and by the way, dear," her mother said. "The Endowment Procedure Ceremony is an evening event this year. Black tie. So you can be dressy."

"Oh, I'll wear the old navy. No problem, Mom. I'd rather save the money for camp. But I'll be happy to go shopping with you and Grandma while you pick something out. It'll be fun."

Juditha laughed. "Yeah, sure."

"No, I mean it, Mom."

In her bedroom before dinner Darci sprawled on the floor and looked at her climbing magazines. She hadn't told her mother the entire truth. One day last summer they had allowed a few of the better climbers to go to a rock face beyond the boulders. By standard levels of difficulty this face would not have ranked high, still, it had opened a world to Darci. Millions of years of erosion had left cracks and fissures that offered up a richness of handholds and toeholds she could never have imagined. It was the randomness that she loved. No computer that designed a climbing gym could ever match it. What intrigued Darci about climbing was that it offered a puzzle for both mind and muscle. One hooked a heel and then reached for a crack overhead, then stemmed out the other foot yearning for a toe wedge, while rotating the knee just so. Your body, your bone, your muscle became an ever-changing piece in the three-dimensional jigsaw puzzle of the rock. She loved it. And when it worked just right there was this feeling of fluid movement. You were part bird, part ballerina. Gravity pulled but you soared, pushing toward a vertical horizon.

In addition to her grandmother being a track star, there had been an uncle who had been a superb college basketball player and a ballerina somewhere on her mother's side, but there had never been a rock climber.

That was what was better in Darci's mind about genetic enhancement when compared to umbellation. Umbellation just copied. It set your destiny completely. But with genetic enhancement things were not so completely set.

Tomorrow there was a class field trip to the Museum of the Reproductive Reformation. The homework for tonight was to come with at least three questions about your own family's gen pro and to seek some information about one of your embryokins.

Like all parents within the last one thousand years, when Darci's parents decided to have a child, not one but several embryos were started through in vitro methods using ova and sperm from Juditha and Leon. The various embryos, or embryokins, were of course screened for any diseases or disabilities, as were the embryos of everyone rich or poor in the Bio Union. Preimplantation genetic diagnosis had come into its golden age in the last four hundred years. Linked with the invention of the forty-eighth chromosome, it offered a previously unimaginable genetic horizon that stretched endlessly in its potential for the development of wonderful skills and talents within a human being.

Now because Juditha and Leon were Genhants there was a wealth of these gifts that they could elect to have within these embryos and to pack onto the forty-eighth chromosome according to their personal tastes and inclinations, as long as they did not violate the Statutes of Traits Selection or the Vanity Laws. There were several virtual Darcis before there was the real Darci. These virtual Darcis were not copies, or umbulae. They were more like sisters or sometimes brothers, and they of course had various combinations of the genetic material of Darci's ancestors. These related embryos, or embryokins as they were called, were kept in cryogenic safety deposit boxes at a Bio Union bank for possible Murlowe children in the future.

One embryokin might be very musical and mathematical but with few athletic skills and possibly high strung with MTD (mild temper disorder), another might be a poet with the ability to master many languages and a gift for humor but slightly shy and maybe even lazy. If material from more than one of the several embryos growing in vitro could be teased apart and then recombined before implantation, parents could possibly have a musical, mathematically gifted poet without MTD or shyness.

Of course no single embryo, even with recombined materials, was perfect, and not even the theoretically perfect embryos were always what reproductive geneticists termed as bioharmonic. In short, they might not hang together on a very basic molecular level and could actually fall apart in vitro before implantation in the womb. A viable embryo therefore was composed of the different embryonic materials from embryokins that had been pulled apart and glued back together again to go into the one embryo that was implanted, which grew into the fetus that eventually grew into the baby that was born and called Darci Murlowe.

Darci now took out her notebook and tapped her teeth with her pencil. What would be her first question about her own embryokins as related to her family gen pro? What about all those other almost-Darcis?

"Mom!" she yelled downstairs.

"Yeah?"

"What's the name of that great-great-aunt who was a ballet dancer—she wasn't a Murlowe, was she?" Darci heard her mom's footsteps coming up the stairs

"No. My side. Her name was Fern Abswith." Undoubtedly some of Fern Abswith's genetic material had become involved in the embryokins that contributed to Darci. So she wrote her first question:

"Was Fern Abswith good in math?" Because Darci definitely wasn't.

"What else do you need to know?" her mother asked.

"I don't know. I'm just supposed to come up with some questions for our field trip tomorrow to the Museum of Reproductive Reformation."

"Like?" her mom asked.

"Well, what were the other embryokins like—any math geniuses frozen up there?"

"Oh, gosh." Juditha looked down and scuffed at something on the carpet with her toe and scratched the back of her neck. "Gee, you're really doing some fairly advanced work, I guess. I don't think we got to embryokin analysis until I was at least a ninth or tenth grader."

"Times have changed," Darci said matter-of-factly. "So how come I didn't get more math smarts? You've certainly got them. What were the other embryokins like?"

"I don't know. I can't remember."

"Can't remember? Mom!"

"Well, I'd have to get the paperwork." Juditha paused and scratched her head. "Gosh, this must be a very accelerated course."

"Any that weren't bioharmonic?"

"Probably a few."

"Probably?" Darci was finding her mother's answers very unsatisfactory. Juditha seemed caught in some edgy place between elaborate disinterest and jittery fear. She tried yawning. It was a fake yawn. "Think I'll head on to bed. I'm really tired."

"Mom!" Darci said. Juditha stopped, alert to the unusual sharpness in her daughter's voice.

"Yeah?" she said, looking at Darci over her shoulder.

"Why me, Mom?"

"What do you mean?" Juditha's face turned pale.

Darci didn't see how it could be much clearer. "I mean, why me? You and Dad probably started—what, ten or twelve different embryokins? Why me and not another—you know, Murlowe embryo number four?"

Juditha's face crinkled into her usual merry smile. "Oh, I don't know, sweetie. I guess we just thought you had that special something!" Then she practically ran out of Darci's bedroom.

"Well, that was helpful!" Darci muttered. She got up and went into her bathroom for her usual before-bed ritual. She leaned over the sink close to the mirror and examined her face for new zits. Except this time she suddenly cocked her head quickly with a flick just as she had seen the kids at Malben's do. Then she raised her right hand toward her face and tried that quick little shake. Not quite right. She tried it again. Better. It wasn't the hand; it was the fingers. They almost quivered. It reminded her of birds ruffing up their feathers just before flight. Imagine if Marilyn Hammertz caught her right now trying to imitate an Original. Or her own parents! Otherness! They'd think she'd gone crazy. Mild Temper Disorder. Should have gone with Murlowe embryo #8.

Chapter 7

"HAVE YOU EVER NOTICED THAT EVERY time we go on a field trip to BOG or like now, to the Museum of the Reproductive Reformation, that they always drive by the Incinerarium?" Max Lasovetch spoke barely above a whisper, but both Darci and Pearl, who shared a seat with him, heard. Indeed the din, the lively chatter on the school bus had suddenly been swallowed up as it turned the corner onto Watson Avenue. The dark profile of the building rose now like a giant gray slab against the sky. Attached to the slab was a series of squat buildings that housed GENPOL, the Agency for Genetic Policing. There was a prison as well. But the central building was the Incinerarium, where violators of the most serious of genetic reproduction laws were executed.

Before the Congress of Reproductive Genetic Law there had been a lawless time when there were absolutely no limits on umbellation or trait selection. It was an era when there had been promiscuous use of genetic material. A black market had developed in the DNA trade of certain star athletes. Indeed this sort of willy-nilly umbellation had actually resulted in killing competitive sports for almost two centuries. New sports had to be developed because watching a team composed entirely of umbulae of 'Lectric Swanson, Eldred Wilmont, and the like—all-star basketball players of the previous millennium—became very boring.

But it was not only in sports that unauthorized umbellation took its toll. There were other fields as well. Finally the Congress came up with the cornerstone legislation for all reprogenetic law. It was during this congress that the Vanity Laws were written, that the Board of Trait Selection and other agencies were established, as well as special courts of law to weigh evidence and mete out punishment. Breaking the Vanity Laws could mean a long prison term, but unauthorized umbellation was the highest crime that could be committed in the Bio Union. The violators were summarily executed along with the umbulae. The executions were always public and televised. The last execution had been nearly ten years before. Darci supposed that her parents had watched it on television but she had been too young to remember.

As soon as they had driven past the Incinerarium, the chatter started up again. A lot of the talk, at least among the girls, centered on what they would be wearing for the Endowment Procedure Ceremony. Every Zolnotz child above the age of ten had been invited. Juditha had been right—the Bio Union was playing the umbellation of the first Zolnotz for all it was worth.

"I'm going to wear a kind of cocktail dress," Marilyn Hammertz was saying, "and spike heels."

"An eighth grader in a cocktail dress. Give me a break!" Pearl muttered.

"What are you wearing, Max?" Darci asked.

He blinked. "What?" His eyes had a distant look as if he were some other place entirely.

"What are you wearing to the Endowment Procedure Ceremony?"

"I haven't even thought about it. Whatever my mom tells me. Why would I care?" He sank back into his seat. He didn't want to talk. Darci could tell. He was still thinking about the Incinerarium.

Why *did* they always go by it? It was out of the way. Must have added twenty minutes on to the trip. Before they had passed by it Darci had been so content just thinking about camp. Indeed that was all she had thought about since her parents both agreed last night that she could go. She had been mentally reviewing the list of climbing gear the brochure said would be required. There was all sorts of fascinating equipment. Equipment that helped a climber to negotiate every pitch and crack, to grip, to wedge a toe, to dance across, up, down, and over rock. That was what she had been thinking about—beautiful rock, granite, sandstone, limestone, each special, all under the arch of a blue sky. And then when she had looked up, there it was—the iron gray slab of steel and concrete—the Incinerarium.

"Welcome, students. Welcome to the Museum of the Reproductive Reformation, the most extensive and biggest museum of its kind in the Bio Union. I know that you have all been here before."

"Like, every year," Max muttered.

"And we try each time to build on your previous experiences here, to add on to the biotech and reprogenetic curriculum that you are following in your classrooms. So we hope that each time you come here your visit will be a little richer, a little more exciting, and most important—I say this to all groups whether they are first graders or eighth and ninth graders like yourselves—to me as the museum director it is not the answers that you come away with but the questions you asked. Questions, not answers, are the basis of all great science. It was questions that led to the great Reproductive Reformation that began in the second half of the twentieth century, over a thousand years ago. So, welcome, kids. Mary Louise here"—he gestured toward a slender black woman—"and I shall be your guides. We have scheduled you today to spend the majority of your time in the computer labs. We have terminals reserved for all of you. So if you'll just follow Mary Louise and myself . . . and remember, pipe up whenever you have a question."

As the children settled behind the terminals to which they had been assigned, the director began to speak again. "This is the central data processing center for the genome. As you all know, we have had the genome, the map that sequences the complete set of human genes, since the early part of the twenty-first century. But did you know"—he began to dim the lights—"that for easy reference and to give better lighting on your computer screen, we also have this map right above your heads." Suddenly a constellation seemed to burst onto the domed ceiling above them with millions of twinkling lights. "This sacred map known as the human genome has been transcribed by lighting experts and artists onto our very ceiling. You will find the forty-eighth chromosome has been illuminated in gold lights. Easy to pick out from the others, although all are labeled. So if you want to take a quick look at, say, the fourteenth chromosome, or let's say the twenty-first, the one worked on so brilliantly by Edmar Golenc—" A chorus of hurrahs swelled up from the children. "Yes indeed, the first Zolnotz. How many Zolnotz children do we have here today? Can we have a show of hands?" Twenty or more hands shot up. "Well, it's something that you can be mighty proud of, kids. We're planning a whole new exhibit here for Edmar, as we do for each of our new Endowment Laureates.

"But for now let's get to the business at hand. You have all, I believe, brought questions about your embryokins. With the computer technology at your fingertips you have the capacity to go back and find out the actual DNA of an embryokin and where its material appears on your own gen pro. But even more interesting, if you have something that matches what, for example, you suspect to be your uncle Harry's profile—say your uncle Harry was a wonderful violinist or maybe a superb basketball player known for his jumping—well, we can get your uncle Harry's genetic profile. Just type it in and you've got it all there before you.

"But before you start I want to say this one thing, and it has to do with our great Bio Union and indeed, why it is so great. We live in a place and at a time when there is real choice. There is no such thing as an unwanted child in the Bio Union. There is no such thing as an 'accident.'" There was a murmuring among the students. "Yes," the director continued. "It is an odd word, isn't it, 'accident,' but that is what the Ancients often called unplanned pregnancies or unplanned babies. Accidents." There was a ripple of laughter throughout the room. "The Ancients did not have any of the choices that we have today. If an embryo was defective they had to either fix it or eliminate it entirely. And they weren't so great at fixing it back then. So it was bye-bye."

"Oooh, yeeech." Several children made a disgusting sound in the backs of their throats.

"That's so pathetic!"

"Gee, they must have been barbaric!"

The director paused while the children muttered in revulsion and then resumed speaking. "There was once a term for this—*abortion*. It is a word no longer in our vocabulary, but if you would go up to Palmyra and the Library of Dead Language you might find it. Abortion is no longer an issue. We do not kill embryos in our culture. There is no need to. Most of the diseases that plagued embryos have been eliminated through genetic engineering. There is no need to select against certain traits. We only need to select for the positive traits but never for . . ." He paused and cupped his hand to his ear waiting for a response.

"The Vanities!" the children all called out robustly.

"Right you are! We can really be *for* something and

this is what our great Bio Union is all about. Being for something, not against it. And it is right here that you can trace the path of all those great genes that each and every one of you have and that have been enhanced through the splendid process of embryonic recombination. Being Genhants—and I want you to listen carefully to this, kids—yes, I know it means that you come from a privileged background that allowed your families to utilize this technology. The other side of the coin is that there are those less fortunate who were not able to afford the enhancement therapies and could only be promised disease-free embryos. But the really important thing is that Bio Union has never told us what we must or must not do in terms of genetic enhancement, except for the basic embryonic inoculation program and the law against the Vanities, and of course unauthorized umbellation. I say the words 'of course,' but I think it bears repeating why unauthorized umbellation is the highest crime in our Bio Union. It is because umbellation is a sacred act, a kind of trust in a sense, by which we preserve and perpetuate the very best of the character and the qualities on which our Union is based. To allow this process to occur in a wild or promiscuous manner would not simply dilute the effects but would be a profanity, an offense to our sense of Otherness. The enhancement therapies are indeed controlled *not* by the Bio Union but by private industry. If you have the money, you can put together any kind of embryo you want."

"SB," muttered Max.

Darci turned her head and looked at him. "What do you mean?" She mouthed the words.

He leaned over and whispered, "Any kind of embryo you want? Come on, Darci, what if you want Original material?"

"Yeah, but there's not a law against it," she whispered back.

"There might as well be one. Those Genhant-Original couples are all but exiled along with the other Bio Rads to the Federation Lands."

Darci supposed Max was right. She remembered vaguely hearing people discuss in hushed voices Genhants and Originals who had fallen in love and married. There were no precise laws against it, but it did seem that these people had a difficult time with everything from schooling for their children to mortgages for houses. They were essentially outcasts. They just didn't fit in.

She listened as the director droned on. "This is the cornerstone of our genetic freedom. It is written into our Bill of Genetic Rights. It is what makes the citizens of this Union and the Union itself the highest form of civilization. We have choice here! This is the Cradle of Genetic Democracy. Now, let's get started."

They had been working a quarter of an hour when Max Lasovetch groaned. "I can't believe how boring my embryokins are," he muttered.

"They can't be that boring, Max. You're pretty weird," Darci offered.

"Oh, I think I'm on the track of my zits." Pearl sighed.

"Oh, my Otherness!" Marilyn Hammertz was exclaiming. "I can't believe Grandfather Rudy's brother, my great-great-uncle. Oh, and their sister . . . Fabulous. My parents were absolutely brilliant in their selection of embryonic material."

"I think I'm going to vomit," Darci whispered.

Marilyn continued, "All my embryokins shared the gene for physics and that is directly out of the Hammertz profile."

"What about your mother's side? Wasn't she included?"

"Of course. That's my artistic side," Marilyn said smugly. "What about you, Max, anything interesting?"

"A poet and an in-line skater—all in one."

"Oh, that's interesting." But her voice was dull as she stared into the computer screen, and Max and Darci both realized that she had hardly heard him. She was much too caught up in her own dazzling genetic history.

Once again they took the extra twenty minutes to go down Watson Avenue and pass by the Incinerarium. And once again an eerie quiet descended upon the bus.

Then when they turned the corner the chatter rose and Darci heard Max say softly, "What if it were just a crapshoot?"

"What are you talking about?" Darci asked.

"What if there were no such thing as embryokins and enhancement therapies, and you just had to take what you got?"

"You mean like before two thousand years ago, or before the Reformation?"

"Yeah."

"It would be like being an Original, I guess."

"No, I mean even the diseases—you might get them," Max said, and looked directly at Darci.

"It would be terrible."

"I think it might be exciting."

"Max, don't be an idiot. It wouldn't be exciting if you had been born with that awful disease from ancient times, cystic fibrosis, where you had to fight for every breath, or Down's syndrome, where you had the mental capacity of a six-year-old. Look, I know this is no real comparison, but when I was a baby I had stronichylimia. I nearly died and was left with a weakened right ankle and foot. I had to wear braces. I still have to do exercises. The exercises were painful at first but I did them faithfully. Now except for my foot size the doctor says you would never know I had the disease. But still, it was no picnic and that was nothing compared to these other things they used to have."

"And what embryokin gave you the will to do your exercises faithfully?" Max turned and asked her. At first Darci thought he was being just plain snotty. But then she realized he was serious. Max had these crystal clear blue eyes, and in this moment she felt as if she were seeing to the very bottom of the deepest lake in the world. "Darci, don't you ever want to be just you—not some pasted-up concoction glued together out of the hopes and dreams of others?"

It was such a peculiar question, such an astonishing thought at the very heart of the question that Darci simply could not speak. There was something overwhelming about the notion of being totally free born. Before the great era of Reproductive Reformation, human babies developed without the benefit of diagnostic embryonic testing or genetic enhancement were called free borns. She wasn't even sure what the term really meant in this sense. To be disease-free was a good thing. But free born seemed ominous, fraught with dangers. So why would they use a word that had always meant good things and positive things for children who could die or be born crippled? But with Max's question came the ghost of another. If you were free born, yes, there was risk, but even risk worked both ways. There were maybe undreamed-of chances. This was truly exciting. Everything in her own life so far had been so explainable, so predictable. She would never, for example, be a great or even an adequate musician. Music and musical ability was simply not really part of the Murlowe's family gen pro; it was not thought to be sufficient to justify music as part of her core educational plan. Every Genhant's educational master plan was worked out through one's parents and the school. One's core educational plan was designed around the dominant traits as expressed in the family gen pro. So Darci could take music, it was not forbidden, but her parents would have to pay extra for it since it was not in her basic individualized curriculum plan. One did not have to delve far into her gen pro to see exactly the reason behind her educational plan.

Darci had looked up her great-grandfather Murlowe, the language scientist, in her embryokin scan and had isolated the bit of genetic material they shared. It certainly did explain her interest in words. Embryokin #3 was very close to her in genetic composition. The main difference seemed to be that it had more of a mathematical inclination, but there seemed to be nothing of Fern Abswith's genetic material in embryokin #3, which probably had zero athletic ability. Darci supposed if her parents got too scared about her rock climbing they could put embryokin #3 into development.

Darci went to sleep that night thinking about what Max had asked her. She looked out her window. A constellation was rising in the sky. A cold, unsettling thought suddenly hit her. She blinked. The stars blurred. What did it matter what she did? If her entire life had been mapped out, why did anything matter? The result would be the same. Except Max had asked her where the will to do her exercises came from, as if he thought it was something unpredictable. Could it be? Was there anything unpredictable in her? Probably not. Even this will was most likely traceable within the gen pro. There was something overwhelmingly depressing about this. To know exactly everything about yourself and what you will ever be—why even bother being born? What was the point of life?

That night Darci dreamed a strange dream of a little embryo. Every time one of the preimplantation genetic probe needles came close, the little embryo shuddered and scuttled around the petri dish. "No, no!" it cried, just trying to buy a little time for another cell division. If it reached the magic number it was too late for the probes. No more genetic material from other embryokins could be added, nor could any be taken away. "Only sixteen more divisions to go," a squeaky little voice said. "Home free!"

Chapter 8

Darci thought her father looked so handsome in his tux. In fact, Darci had to admit her whole family looked terrific. Her mother had chosen a gold-colored dress with an overlay of pale green lace and a beautiful embroidered shawl. Grandma Venka was dressed in a pewter gray satin that was several shades darker than her own light gray hair. She wore an antique necklace with little ruby chips woven into a web of silver. Darci herself wore the pink mesh dress with the appliquéd flowers. Even though she was going to camp her mother said she needed something special. They were all here to honor Edmar Golenc—camp or no camp.

The Murlowes followed the streams of people into

The Academy of Endowment, a beautiful building in the early Reproductive Reformation style with soaring towers, slender archways, and gleaming steel tracery. They walked through the entryway and then were guided across an interior courtyard to the Tabernacle of Endowment. Ushers took their invitations, which were coded for seating, and directed them. Darci hoped they would get a good seat. Her father said the best seats were actually not on the main floor but up in the gallery, which afforded a better view. Darci flashed her dad an excited little grin when it became apparent that they were being directed to go up the stairs to the first gallery.

"How about this, Venka?" Leon mouthed the words to his mother. The seats had to be the best in the Tabernacle. They could look directly down into the Sanctum of Bestowal where the Endowment Laureates would sit and the procedure would be carried out. There were twenty gilt chairs for the Laureates. Facing them, a group of thirty chairs for the CERA, the Central Endowment Regulatory Agency, and the BOS, the Board of Selection executive council members. It was these two administrative groups that oversaw the nominations of the candidates for Endowment and gave final approval. At the very head of the Sanctum was the Throne of the Primarchy. On one side of the throne was a smaller throne for the Prima Matri, the present Prima's predecessor, the thirty-first copy of the first Prima. She was not exactly a "mother" in the true biological sense, for although she had given birth to the present Prima she was technically her identical older twin, her umbula. For it was the thirty-first Prima from whom the thirty-second had been umbellated. The Prima Matri always abdicated on her fiftieth birthday, when the new Prima became twenty. The Prima Matri was now a woman of sixty.

There was a sound of bugles. This was the signal that the ceremony was about to begin. The audience rose for the procession of the Prima. First came the Grenadiers of the Bio Union, an elite Primerial Guard whose forbears had fought brilliantly at the Battle of Rosebeth Field against the madman dictator of the Union of Zuane, which had attempted to seize genetic material from the Bio Union and hold it for ransom some three hundred years before. Between the two columns of the Grenadiers walked the twenty new Endowment Laureates. Darci spotted Edmar Golenc immediately. His thick brush of wiry hair flared like a white bonfire from his head. Her father nudged her and pointed down at his mentor. Darci nodded and smiled.

But now she felt her heart thumping. She was about to see the Prima. Darci had never in her life seen her in person this close up. The two columns of Grenadiers seemed endless, but then there was a drumroll and a shrill blast on the trumpets. A rustling and creaking filled the Tabernacle as over one thousand people kneeled. Luckily the guardrail in the gallery where the Murlowes sat had widely spaced spindles. Darci could look right down through them. There was the gleaming head of the Prima, directly beneath her. The gown the Prima wore glittered with tens of thousands of small glistening jewels and pearls. Darci thought of the sparkling ceiling at the Museum of the Reproductive Reformation bristling with the constellations of the genome. The Prima was not a mere constellation. She was an entire galaxy.

She mounted the stairs to the Sanctum of Bestowal and took her seat on the throne. Beside her sat the Prima Matri. From this distance they looked absolutely identical. One could not see the older woman's wrinkles. She held herself erect and proud. The lighting in the Tabernacle erased any visible differences between the younger and the elder woman's hair, although one was blonde and the other silvery white. Darci saw the Prima Matri lean over and speak to the Prima. The Prima nodded and the Prima Matri smiled sweetly. Darci wondered what they were talking about. She suddenly noticed Max Lasovetch down below. He looked totally bored. In fact—Darci was shocked—he looked as if he had fallen asleep. He was just too much! How rude. She was relieved when she saw his mom jostle him and give him a very severe look. Serves him right! Darci thought.

There was some more scraping of chairs as the Laureates took their seats. They could not sit before the Prima sat on the Throne of the Primarchy. Then with no further fanfare the Prima began to speak. Her voice seemed thin with a slight quaver at the center. Not nearly as strong as it had sounded on television for the Reading of the Lists.

"Good people of the Bio Union . . . " The speech was the same one she gave every year that Darci had read often in the newspaper. But hearing it now seemed very different. Her voice shook. She had done this so many times, why should she be nervous? She thanked the members of both CERA and BOS for their devotion to duty, their hard work, the thoughtfulness which they brought to this, the most important task of the Bio Union. She complimented them on their extraordinary selection and then, in a departure from the usual speech, spoke of how truly "joyful" she was that during her reign as Prima, the Board of Selection and the Regulatory Agency saw fit to include the first Zolnotz, that she hoped that throughout the years other Zolnotz endowments would follow. Her voice became steadier. "We live in a Union of indescribably rich genetic diversity and the best way to celebrate this diversity is through umbellation of the outstanding men and women from some of the minority ethnic groups like Zolnotz." But again, her voice seemed to crack as she spoke the word "umbellation."

Now the actual procedure would begin. The Prima rose from her throne, flanked by members from both CERA and BOS, each carrying a tray with the Implements of Endowment. There was a Grenadier to assist in the handing of the implements. The Laureates remained seated as the Prima approached. On one tray glistened sixteen slender, curved, scoop-shaped instruments, curettes, for scraping the flesh of the interior wall of each Laureate's mouth. On the second tray sixteen vials rested encased in small battery-powered thermoses. The curettes with their sample scrapings containing the cells for umbellation would be plunged into the vials, which had been cooled to the critical temperature.

The Laureates were arranged in alphabetical order. The first Laureate was Josephine Allarck, a composer and conductor who had actually created a new musical scale. Darci watched as the woman, near seventy now, dropped her mouth wide open for the Prima to insert the curette. It was a totally painless procedure. There was no cutting. A simple swipe was all that was needed. The Prima then turned to the man bearing the tray of thermoses and quickly plunged the curette into the thin vial. Darci's father had explained that the vials were hermetically sealed before the insertion of the curette and that a sealant immediately formed around the stem of the instrument when it was placed in the vial. The Prima turned back to a beaming Josephine Allarck, leaned down, and kissed her on each cheek. Darci tried to imagine what this moment might feel like. It was completely unimaginable to her. Yes, it was the highest honor one could ever achieve on earth. But how strange to imagine that within hours after the ceremony this collection of cells would be placed in a nucleus-free ova and then given an electrical impulse, triggering a synthetic fertilization event, which in turn would lead to the first cellular divisions of the next Josephine Allarck. They would not share life on the earth for very long. No one could become a Laureate until he or she was at least sixty-five.

The Prima now moved on to the next Laureate. Darci checked her program. Horatio Dybolt, an astrophysicist, for his work on gamma ray synthesization. Darci had no idea what gamma ray synthesis was about. Very possibly something to do with energy. There were two more Laureates before Edmar Golenc. When his turn came Darci watched, mesmerized, as his immense head with the uncontrollable thatch of white hair tipped back and he opened his mouth. When had his hair turned white? How old had he been? A horde of embarrassingly stupid thoughts raced through Darci's mind. How would a little kid feel about getting that frizzy, out-of-control hair? His nose was no prize either. These were shameful thoughts—all of them centered on the outlawed Vanities—but she could not keep them from flooding her mind. And Edmar Golenc had never seemed a very happy man. He had never married. His umbula would be raised in a manner identical to that in which Edmar had been raised, and although there was no law that said the umbula could not marry, he probably would not. Golenc's life had been one of pure intellectual devotion. Singleness was the word that most came to mind with Edmar Golenc. He lived alone. He dedicated himself to a single intellectual pursuit—the twenty-first chromosome. He lived in a state of nearly complete singleness except for the very few students whom he nurtured. He had no pets, no hobbies. In his lab he liked to do everything himself and had not the usual staff of technicians save for a very few. It was said that he could go through a day speaking no more than fifty words. He preferred written communication to spoken.

Darci's father had two complete file cabinets, two drawers each, filled with his years of correspondence with Edmar. Still, despite Golenc's lack of social skills, Leon Murlowe felt very close to his longtime mentor and Golenc felt close to Leon and Juditha. Once a year he would come to dinner. He spoke very few words then. Darci remembered how the silence would gather around them as they sat at the dinner table, and yet it never felt awkward. In fact, Darci rather liked it compared to when her parents had other associates for dinner. There was never any small talk with Edmar, no condescending chitchat to make the child feel included, no patronizing questions. He would smile softly at her sometimes. Once she remembered him saying "lovely" about her dress. Another time, "interesting movement" about a clay sculpture of hers she had shown him. And when he had heard about her rock-climbing activities he had asked to see her fingers and for her to show him the crimp grip, a kind of small hold grip. Darci had only read about it herself but tried to demonstrate it. "I think it might stress the knuckles. Use it discreetly," he had said.

So in her entire life Edmar Golenc had spoken perhaps one hundred words to Darci and yet she thought she might be able to remember every single one of them. How many people could you say that about? How many people were there whose every single word really counted in that way? And now there would be another Edmar Golenc. But how would his umbula feel? If he could choose this singleness, would he? Darci thought of what Max Lasovetch had said on the bus coming back from the Museum of the Reproductive Reformation: didn't she ever want to be just herself, not some pasted-up concoction glued together out of the hopes and dreams of others? And, of course, an umbula was many steps further away from a pasted-up concoction. An umbula was an exact copy, a copy of a dream come true, a genius come true. But had anyone ever really dreamed of such a lonely life?

Chapter 9

"COME ON IN, VENKA. COME ON, RUFUS," Darci's mother urged.

"Have a nightcap," said her father as they walked up to the house.

It was as if they couldn't stop celebrating. It was probably the same in Zolnotz houses all over the city, people trying to extend the glory of the moment. Darci wondered if there would be new celebrations nine months from now when the umbula of Edmar Golenc was born.

"Well, why not, Venka? How often is there a day like this?" Darci's grandfather took his wife in his arms and gave her a little twirl up the walk.

"Dancing, he is!" Venka exclaimed. "Do you know how much trouble I usually have getting him out onto the dance floor? When was the last time we danced—maybe our thirtieth wedding anniversary?"

"I'll dance with you tonight."

Five minutes later Darci was perched on a window seat in the living room, watching the grown-ups dance. They looked so weird. She doubted if Edmar Golenc was dancing. "Home to bed!" was the last thing he had said to her father and mother when they left the reception. The more she watched them dance the weirder things began to seem. They are celebrating because a person of our ethnic background, a minority race, has been endowed, Darci mused. She thought of those madly dividing cells. Again Max's words came to haunt her. She wondered what it might have been like thousands of years ago, before the Reformation had really begun, in the time of free borns. She began once more to think about the word "free"—what did it really mean? And the word "original." The more Darci thought about words, about free borns, about the meaning of not just the words but everything, the less sense all of these things seemed to make. The world as she knew it seemed to be disintegrating in front of her very eyes to the tempo of the music as her parents and grandparents bobbed about, as the cells continued their division toward dreams of genius. The music stopped now and the grown-ups settled down onto the two facing sofas.

"Well, quite a day!" Venka sighed.

"How many cell divisions before they implant the embryo of Edmar Golenc's umbula?"

"Sixteen now," her father answered. "So in five days. They used to do it after only three divisions, but that was in the very earliest part of the Reformation. Now they wait."

"Who's the birth mother?" Darci asked.

"Darci! You know better than that. They always keep it very secret." Her mother looked genuinely shocked.

"A Zolnotz?" Darci asked.

"Well, one must assume. They try to replicate as precisely as possible the conditions, the environment in which the Laureate was born and grew up," her mother said, and looked at Darci curiously. At first Darci thought it was that look her mother gave her when she asked an obvious question, as if to say "You know all this, this is very basic. Why are you asking?" But there was something else in her mother's eye. A glimmer of fear?

Her father quickly got up and turned on the music. "Come on, Darci, out onto the dance floor. Anyone who is as agile on rocks as you should be able to drag her old man around the dance floor."

"Dad!" Darci hated this. It was too embarrassing. But she took her father's hand and it was he who did the dragging, or rather the guiding, around the dance floor. He looked down at her and smiled. She could see his gray-blue eyes. The thick lenses of his glasses made them appear slightly smeared. His eyes crinkled at the edges into the familiar smile creases, but did something else flicker within them? She peered a bit harder and he smiled harder. There was something there. "Hey, Darci," he said suddenly. "When are we going to get your equipment for camp? How about tomorrow?"

"Tomorrow? Don't you have to work?"

"I'll leave early."

"You will?"

"Sure, kiddo."

"Oh, Dad."

Now he smiled and the creases deepened and if fear was not there before, a look of relief seemed to sweep across his gray-blue eyes and lighten them behind the thick lenses.

Later in bed Darci sat with a notebook propped against her knees and began her shopping list for camp.

> *two metal snap locks*
> *one full body harness*
> *one helmet*
> *gear loops*

Darci stopped writing and looked at the list of words. She was suddenly struck with how plain and simple the words were. They seemed tangible, like rock itself, with no hidden meanings. They said what they did.

Darci had simply been making a list but now her pen seemed to flow across the page. *I am a Genhant, a genetically enhanced human and a snap lock is a lock that snaps shut or closes quickly. Why do some words say what they do and others don't? A gear loop is simply a loop for hanging gear from your belt. But what is an Original—why do they call an Original an Original?* She stopped writing. Another word stumbled into her mind: *umbula. Why is Edmar Golenc's human copy called an umbula? And what the heck is umbellation? Yes, yes, I know what it is, what the process is. I can see all those cells dividing, copying and copying and copying, but why would they call a copy an umbula? Does the word really mean copy? Or is it a . . .*

Darci stopped writing again and whispered one word: "trick." Is it all a trick, she thought, one big universal cosmic trick, to call things by other names? Maybe it all started out innocently, not really to fool people but just to get them used to something, or maybe it was a code in the beginning, but then somehow the key to the code was lost and over time the meanings of words just evaporated like dew on a flower's petals, like morning mist in a brightening day.

Darci closed the notebook. She knew she would come back to it, that tonight she had begun something. A story? A journal? She was not sure. She could see the edges of the notebook. They seemed to gleam in the light that fell through her bedroom window from the full moon. There was something almost dangerous about the book lying in the small patch of moonlight, daring her . . . daring her to do what?

Chapter 10

Darci could hear the change in the thrumming sound as the BLINK, the Bio Union's Link to the Kerals, a high-speed rail, began to climb. Darci was glad the train would begin to go slower. She could finally watch the landscape, which up to now had been just a blur. Max Lasovetch sat next to her.

"This is definitely the best part of the trip. You won't believe the Kerals. They are beautiful."

"I wish you were going to camp with me instead of to your brother's lab."

"I told you already. I avoid physical exertion."

"There's a mental part to rock climbing."

"Why dilute the mental with the physical if it can be

helped? I'll take my mental stuff full strength, thank you."

Darci looked at him and shook her head. "Max, you're weird."

"So what else is new. Look! Look up and out!"

Darci gasped. They were sitting in a clear plastic capsule on the second tier of the BLINK and when she looked up all she saw were stone curtains—pure white stone curtains. "It's the Palmyra sandstone cliffs, the official entrance into the Kerals and the Arc of the Winds region."

"Oh, my . . . oh, my!" Darci whispered.

"Jillions of years of erosion. They say that the windstorms of the twenty-first century were what put the finishing touches on them—curtained them, so to speak."

And "curtain" was the perfect word, for the cliffs hung in deep draping folds, slightly billowed as if blown by a petrified wind.

"Look, a climber!" Max pointed toward the cliffs. "Up there to the right."

Sure enough, Darci saw a tiny red speck on the convex side of a fold. "I can't believe it. How can a person . . . oh, he's so high, the rocks so smooth . . . how . . ."

"Sure you don't want to dilute your physical with a little more mental?" Max asked.

Darci would have been lying if she did not admit to

experiencing a slightly sinking feeling in the pit of her stomach as she watched the climber on that curtain of rock. But when she looked higher and saw the sky, then out of the corner of her eye caught a glimpse of a peregrine flying lower than the climber, gravity suddenly seemed so silly, so superfluous to her very nature. Forget she was this wingless, earthbound human—she wanted to soar. The only horizon that counted for Darci was vertical. The horizontal, gravity, for a split second seemed as senseless as soil and air for a fish. It was simply not her element.

The BLINK serpentined its way through the stone curtains and then after ten minutes or so the stone curtains began to draw back, revealing a new landscape, one prickly with spires that soared straight up, in many cases over two thousand feet high. In the late afternoon sun these spires cast long skinny shadows that latticed the entire world. Darci looked at Max. His light brown curly hair danced with the light and shadow from the stone spires. The interior of the train became woven with light and shadow.

Within forty-five minutes they had passed through the most amazing array of geological wonders Darci could have ever imagined. As the BLINK pulled into the station Darci turned to Max. "I wish you were going to camp with me. But maybe we'll get to see each other. They said in the letter that we have field trips to a place called the Cascades, which is supposed to be good for swimming. I'll let you know."

"You got my brother's number and all that?"

"Yep."

There were counselors waiting for Darci and the other campers who arrived on the train. Darci was in group eleven, which included one kid from the rock-climbing club in her school. The rest were from other Genhant schools in the capital. Most of them had been to rock-climbing camps before and two, Jessica and Davis, had been to Arc of the Winds. They were older and very good climbers.

Darci waved good-bye to Max and climbed into one of the vans with the rest of her group. The counselors in her van were Arnie and Beth. Beth was the stringiest woman Darci had every seen. Darci thought if you pinched her she might twang just like a guitar. Darci could see that her fingers, long and bony, had a white residue on the tips. Arnie was driving and Beth turned around to talk to the kids. "How'd you like the scenery coming up?"

"Great!"

"Wow!"

"I'll say wow!" Beth laughed. "Well, you know every kind of rock formation you saw you will have had experience climbing on by the end of your session."

"Even the Curtains?" asked a boy named Martin.

"Even the Curtains. Not those Curtains precisely. There are some shorter Curtains near camp, but they go straight up and so will you." She held up her hands now with her fingers splayed apart. "See that white stuff like powder? That's Palmyra sandstone. You'll get a close-up look at it when we pass the Prima's palace. It's made entirely from Palmyra sandstone."

"Is she there now?" a girl named Chloe asked.

"You bet. The Prima spends as much time as possible here. It's her favorite palace of all, especially in the summertime."

They had been in the van less than ten minutes when Beth said, "All right kids, the palace is coming up in the next block."

A glistening white dome rose above an immense spiky green hedge. Other smaller domes began to reveal themselves, floating like bubbles over the twenty-foot-high hedge. As they rounded the corner the hedge was replaced by iron gates and then the palace, in all of its stunning whiteness, revealed itself. It was the same pure white as the sandstone Curtains, but instead of the deep folds of the Curtains, the walls of the palace were scored by thousands of skinny pleats giving the effect of a beautiful sheer fabric like chiffon or silk. A silence fell among the children in the van. Finally one girl, Debbie, asked the question, "How did it get that way—the stone?"

"Not naturally." Arnie laughed. "They would have had to wait for millions of years for the stone to erode to look like the Curtains you saw. No, when the new palace was built in the last century the architects decided to speed up the erosion and developed a water-blasting technique that scoured out these thin folds or pleats. Nice, huh?"

"I'll say," whispered several of the kids.

"Must have cost a mint," said another

"She's *got* a mint," said someone else.

"What is just as spectacular as the sandstone are the gardens. Last year we were invited to a garden party, the entire camp. We're hoping that they'll invite us again this year too!"

"Wow!" exclaimed the campers.

"We've never been invited to anything at the Prima's palace in the capital."

"It's different here," Arnie said

As soon as he said it, Darci, who had felt herself in some sort of odd state of suspended animation, realized the full and overpowering truth of that statement. Everything seemed different here in the Kerals, in the Arc of the Winds. The air was different, the sky, the very earth with its unending variety of rock was all so different she scarcely believed she was on the planet Earth. The strangeness had begun to seep into her as soon as she stepped off the BLINK. And although it felt strange it was not frightening. This was a place full of light. Did it reflect off the white rock and make an unusual brightness? She sensed the coolness of shadows hovering at the edge. Was it the shadows that beckoned? Something seemed to beckon, to call to her, to draw her in more deeply with every breath she took. The voices of the other campers were a meaningless babble in her ears. She was there in the van with her fellow campers, yet she felt somewhat apart. She felt that only she was being drawn to something else within this strange land. She did not know what. And the more she thought about it the more elusive this thing out there was. She didn't want it to run away. It was a good feeling. The only way to keep it seemed to be to stop thinking about it too hard.

"And here we are passing the Library of Dead Language." Darci had been so consumed with her own odd feelings that she nearly missed it as Beth pointed it out. She turned around just in time to see another Palmyra sandstone building, this one unscored by the pleats and made from simple but elegantly carved blocks of the white stone.

In another fifteen minutes they were at the camp. Darci was assigned to a cabin with three other girls, Moira, Rena, and Peggy. Rena and Peggy were best friends and immediately decided where they would sleep—in the upper bunks. They did not even consult

Darci or Moira, who were left with the lower bunks. Indeed they hardly made any attempt at all to speak to Darci and Moira. Rena and Peggy had been to a gymnastics camp together the summer before. They began talking about how gymnastics was the best preparation one could have for rock climbing. They seemed to almost swagger with their gymnastic talk as they blabbed on about various muscle groups and how their fabulous quads or deltoids were perfectly developed for the various moves in rock climbing. Darci hated people who used language and words this way—to impress and ultimately to assault. Words emptied of meaning became dry, brittle husks. Voices whistled through them like shrill winds. Maybe this was how language died.

When they left the cabin to find the bathrooms Darci looked over at Moira, who appeared absolutely miserable sitting by her bedroll.

Darci felt a twinge of real sorrow for her. She looked so pathetic sitting there with her chubby legs bulging out of her shorts. "They might know a lot about quads and deltoids—or delts, as they were saying, but they don't know piss about rock climbing," Darci muttered.

Moira smiled for the first time. "I'm going to be awful at this."

"No, you won't. It's easy. You'll love it."

"I'm fat and I'm scared of heights," Moira said, the misery creeping over her face again.

Darci did not have a quick answer for this. "Why did you come?"

"It was this or fatties camp."

"Fatties camp?" Darci asked.

"Yeah, that's what I call it. Weight loss camp."

"You didn't want to go?"

"I went last year. It was dreadful." Moira shook her head. She had a very pretty face really, and the little black springy ringlets that framed it shivered. "Imagine a camp where all you think about is your body, your weight, what you put in your mouth. And they say it's not competitive. But it is. People are always bragging about how much weight they've lost, or how little they ate, that they did not take the bonus snack, or how they ran two miles to work off some forbidden food that they had sneaked on a trip to town."

"Yeecch!" Darci made a disgusted sound.

"My parents have to pay extra for this—a lot extra."

"Oh, it's not in your gen pro," Darci said.

"Nothing even vaguely related. I mean in my core educational plan for athletics it's been mostly Ping-Pong. Ping-Pong and croquet. I was junior champion in croquet when I was nine."

"Wow!" Darci said.

"Ping-Pong and croquet are okay, but frankly I'm bored. I'm going to be playing Ping-Pong to my dying day. And my aunt and uncle own a croquet resort."

"Gee, I guess rock climbing is sort of a stretch."

"My parents were shocked, but I thought rock climbing just sounded . . . well, I don't know, so . . . so honest, at least compared to fatties camp."

In that moment Darci knew she would be friends, good friends, with Moira.

"You know what I mean?" She looked up at Darci with gray eyes that reminded Darci of the color of tumbling water.

"I think so."

"I mean, I just don't want to spend a summer thinking about me and food and me and calories and me and my weight. It's so . . . so selfish! I just thought me and rock sounded better, even if I am scared of heights. I guess it's ridiculous, given my gen pro and all."

But it made a strange kind of sense to Darci. She looked at this large, plump girl and marveled quietly to herself—Moira just said SB to her entire family gen pro. How daring! How wonderful! She felt almost envious. She wished she could think of something to do completely at odds with her own gen pro, totally unpredictable.

The one good thing about sleeping in the lower bunk was that it seemed very private. Darci could read with her flashlight and write without the light disturbing anyone else. When Rena had her flashlight on the beam bounced off the ceiling and cast a dim sheet of light on the walls. But Darci felt as if she were in a dark honey-lit cocoon. She took out her notebook. She had not written in it since the night of the Endowment Ceremony. She read the last sentences.

Why is Edmar Golenc's human copy called an umbula? And what the heck is umbellation? Yes, yes, I know what it is, what the process is. I can see all those cells dividing, copying and copying and copying but why would they call a copy an umbula? Why umbellation? Does the word really mean copy? Or is it a . . .

She forgot what she had intended to say, but now Moira's words came back to her: "I thought rock climbing was so honest by comparison." Darci began to write. *Ever since I have arrived here in the Kerals I have had the strangest feelings. Arnie said this is a different place and I know he is right, but I am not sure how it is different. It certainly feels different, but when Moira said about rock climbing being honest . . . I don't know*

The thing that she had sensed in the van out there somewhere waiting for her began to slip away again. But she hadn't been thinking about IT. She had been thinking about Moira and what Moira had said. She thought she had felt alone and apart. She did. But she sensed, no, she knew, that Moira felt the same way too. But this was not why she felt close to Moira. It was not because they both felt apart and therefore were in some crazy way together. It was something else.

Darci had turned off her flashlight. Moira was still reading, propped up on one elbow. She had strung her flashlight to the bottom of the bunk overhead. A cone of light shown down on the book and her right hand, which held it open. Moria's head and shoulders were outside the cone of light, but Darci could see how intent Moira was on her reading. Suddenly, like the flutter of a bird lifting into flight, something beat at the edge between the cone of light and the pool of darkness. It was Moira's hand. It shivered perfectly, just like the kids at Malben's.

Chapter 11

"THIS IS ALL ABOUT TRUST," DAVE, THE bouldering counselor, was saying. "I don't care how good your gear is, how deft your footwork, how strong you are. In fact, being a good climber has more to do with movement than with strength. It really gets down to how creative you are on that rock face, but first you've got to have trust. The exercises we're going to do out here on Little Baldy are all designed to teach you that trust. You're going to learn how to spot for your buddies and your buddies to spot for you.

"Okay, Jessica and Davis know this from last summer. So why don't you two step up and then Beth and Arnie. I'm going to climb up on this stump, which is only—

what, three feet off the ground?" Darci watched as the four people he called up gathered around. "On the count of three or maybe five or who knows—" Suddenly Dave fell backward. Jessica, Davis, Arnie, and Beth caught him, breaking his fall.

For the next forty-five minutes they divided into groups and practiced a series of trust falls. Some were as simple as pushing one person back and forth between two others; some were falling off the stump or low parts of the Little Baldy boulder.

Darci could have killed Rena and Peggy when they were doing the trust pushes with Moira. They were snickering and rolling their eyes the entire time, and when Moira was barely out of earshot they made a snide comment about her weight and how squishy she was. Darci was furious. She turned and hissed, "How can you be so cruel? What do you have for brains, deltoids?" The two girls shrugged and walked off.

Next they learned about spotting, which was like the trust exercises except now they were actually on the boulder and one person stood at the base behind the climber with his or her hands up, thumbs tucked ready to catch the climber in case of a fall. Moira spotted Darci and Darci spotted Moira. Moira did slip once and Darci was right there to catch her. In that moment something soared out of Darci—a strength, a feeling—and she was not even aware of Moira feeling heavy or light or anything. She was just Moira.

They spent the rest of the morning "bouldering," practicing various moves within a low and safe range. By afternoon they had moved on to some more difficult moves but still in the low, safe range of Little Baldy. The boulder routes were called boulder problems. Darci liked the term. You had to search for the lines, the cracks, the angles, and estimate the stretch of your leg or the reach of your arm. Darci noticed that although Moira was heavy she had tiny and very flexible feet. They seemed sometimes to simply melt into the rock, so even though her mobility and stretch were not that great her feet made up for a lot. She thought again about Moria's hands, how the left one had fluttered in the darkness. Maybe Moira hung out at a place like Malben's. Maybe she secretly found something attractive and compelling about the way in which Originals moved their heads and hands. Darci smiled to herself and thought of the night she had tried it in front of the mirror. She hadn't been half bad.

By midmorning of her second day at camp Darci felt that Dave and Beth and Arnie were watching her quite a bit. Just after she had completed some very tricky footwork to cross a particularly smooth pitch of the boulder, she heard the words, "Beautiful, Darci! I think you're ready to go higher for some top roping. Right after lunch, okay?"

"Okay."

An hour later Darci was in her body harness and plastered to the side of the granite slab.

She was breathing hard. She couldn't see a crack or whisker of an edge to crimp on to. Her eyes slid across the rock. She spotted one fairly decent crack, but her leg would have had to grow at least another three inches and then she could use a foot the size of Moira's. A new body, that's what she needed—*some pasted-up concoction glued together out of the hopes and dreams of others?*

"What am I supposed to do now?" she yelled.

"You figure it out," Dave called back. "You make the moves."

"I make the moves," Darci muttered. She looked about again. She felt that she had come to know this rock face too well; that it could not, or perhaps refused to, yield up anything new to her. She had stared for endless minutes at the golden embroidery of lichen that was just inches from her nose. To the right of her head and just above flecks of mica glittered in a taunting calligraphy—a secret language perhaps? A hidden meaning? But why would this rock reveal its meaning to her? Why would it surrender meaning any more readily than the words that seemed also to taunt her with such constancy? Why was she always looking for meaning in everything? It was as if she had been born not quite human but existed instead as some sort of living probe, a sonar creature whose fate it was to be confounded by signs and symbols that never were in alignment with true meaning. She was like a compass out of whack, the needle swaying wildly between the true north of the real geography of the country and the magnetic north of the poles.

She leaned back what seemed like a foot but was just a matter of inches, and saw a tiny edge, no bigger than a row of baby's teeth. It was a crimp grip. She was careful to stack her thumb over her forefinger as she had been taught to add strength to the grip and reduce stress. It worked. She could now inch herself over toward the lovely crack that beckoned as tempting as a glass of ice water on the hottest day, as bread to a starving person, soup to a . . . Darci's mind seemed to be working on two levels. She never remembered concentrating on anything so hard in her life. And yet as these images of food or drink tripped through her mind, her famished mind, she knew it was not really food she craved. It was a grip, a hold, a crack, a wedge. She edged toward the crack, closing the distance in minutes that seemed to stretch as long as afternoons.

Chapter 12

THE HOURS OF CLIMBING SLIPPED INTO days, and the days into weeks. Darci learned to climb on granite and sandstone and scree slopes littered with broken rocky debris that could slide out instantly from under her feet. Her eyes became alert to every kind of fissure and crevice. She had jammed herself into cracks a foot or more in width known as chimneys, and shimmied upward in them as high as seventy-five feet. She had knotted her hand into fist cracks that were only three or four inches wide and wedged herself upward. She had slithered her arm into a six-inch crack, bending it chicken wing style, to hold and brace herself, then cranked herself higher by pushing with her feet. Every move Darci learned seemed to have one goal: to keep a climber stuck to the surface. Essentially this meant playing opposing forces against one another. If your hands pulled, your feet pushed.

By the end of the third week she had learned to hang upside down on the underside of overhangs, the sections of a rock wall that jut out abruptly, luring climbers into a reverse world in which feet swing above their heads and work like hands. While most climbing is done on a vertical plane, overhang climbing transpires on the horizontal. A climber is on his or her back, so to speak, pressed between rock and thin air. Darci had practiced overhang moves on low rocks for four days solid. She had become obsessed with what the counselors called "dynos," in which a climber was required to make a very long reach on an overhang and then propelled the rest of his or her body to a new position on the rock. This was accomplished by grabbing a single good hold with both hands and then running one's feet high. At the point of maximum height the climber boosted herself into a kind of leap. At this point, the dead point, the moment when the climber is weightless and ready to drop, he or she must let go with one hand and make a grab for a higher hold.

Darci was readjusting her harness on a low overhang at the end of an afternoon when Arnie and Beth came over to her.

"Darci," Beth said. "We think you're ready for the Greybeards."

"The Greybeards!" Darci gasped. Everyone talked about the Greybeards. They were a formation of rocks, close to camp, that offered everything from granite spires to endless overhangs and curtains of Palmyra sandstone. Within one climb a person could encounter at least three different kinds of rock and go from crack climbing, or jamming, to huge expanses of smooth rock without so much as a wrinkle, to eerie multitiered white overhangs.

That night as Darci lay in her bed thinking about the Greybeards she felt a mixture of excitement and fear. Once more the strangeness she had first experienced when arriving in the Kerals swept through her. The strangeness was linked somehow with a growing sense of apartness. The apartness was peculiar. She suddenly realized that she had felt it on some level for a long time, from a time long before she had ever even thought of coming to the Kerals and the Arc of the Winds. Perhaps she had somehow denied it, or maybe the feelings had been masked by something else. Her friendship with Moira had probably done the most to divert her from thinking about it. She never felt apart when she was with Moira. And she bet it would be the same if she were with Max, but there had been no time to go see him so far.

Every day she felt closer to Moira and yet she knew

she was being pulled elsewhere. The feeling came to her like a dim current in a stream; there was that sense of subtle motion, of being urged, coaxed, beckoned toward an unknowable, unnameable thing. And yet she had somewhere in her brain known this thing from long ago, or known this feeling. It did not surprise her. But it was here in the Kerals that she had perhaps dared to let herself feel it. Darci quietly got out her notebook and began to write.

Yesterday I climbed a pretty good overhang. I "dynoed," as they say, one very difficult part. Dyno means dynamic climbing—reaching, grabbing—quick powerful grabs, spurts with feet and arms. It basically says what it is. I think that is what I most like about this place and what I am doing. The words, the rocks, the moves are what they are. Rock faces aren't for liars. There is simply no lying on a rock face. You jam, you crimp, you wedge, you crank, you do a heel hook. Dead point is a point of weightlessness in time. You are virtually between earth and sky. You are borne by air. You are all and you are nothing within one millionth of a second. It is an extraordinary point in time. It happens between heartbeats. I like it here, in this rocky heaven on earth, in which all is as it was made and even language seems as solid as the rocks we climb. And yet I do believe that although there are no lies, there are secrets, mysteries. Am I the only one who feels this? Is this why I feel sometimes, even when I am with Mo, so alone, so apart?

This time IT did not flee. And Darci now suspended herself in that moment of feeling IT's nearness, and she wondered if once upon a time the whole world was another way and knew this thing of which she was just beginning to sense glimmerings.

Darci yawned. The night was moonless and the darkness pressed in upon her, thick and seemingly impenetrable. But it was a comfort. Darci opened her eyes wide. Nothing was evenly black, or for that matter evenly white, she thought. There were shadows within the blackness of this night, and shadows within the shadows, some as thin as veils, others dense and opaque. You could see the gleam of a blackbird's wing in a night like this. You had to try, though. You had to train your eye to see the dark shapes, black against the black, the gray within the shadows, the design of the earth's night against the blackness of the universe. Darci lifted her hand and fluttered it. She smiled to herself in the darkness. She heard Rena sigh and turn over. The mattress above her creaked. She let the blackness of this night fill her, creep into her, lay its dark fingers upon her eyelids. She was alone and drifting on the dark billows of a silky night sea.

A door came to Darci that night in her dreams. At first there was just the wall, a rock wall. Darci was in her harness looking for the cracks, the tiny crimp ledges, but then she found the lines, straight as seams, the precise geometry, the right angles so rare in nature. She knew in an instant that there was a door in that rock but then that vertical rock face vanished and she was hanging upside down under an overhang. The door must be here, she kept thinking. What a nifty way to negotiate an overhang—literally go through it instead of out and over the edge. She could feel the grit under her fingertips as she searched for the familiar lines, the ones she had seen before, but suddenly she was falling. *You idiot, how can you be doing this hanging upside down on an overhang?* a voice screamed in her head. *Your hands are your feet; tiptoe your fingers across the rock and you plummet.* Then it began. She was plummeting to her death, and in an instant another door suddenly opened. She saw it so clearly, a door in the beautiful blue sky, between thin air and sky—a door!

Darci did not know how long she had slept but she woke into the thin gray light of near dawn. It was as if the skin of the night had been pulled back and the bones of the new day were just revealing themselves. Darci remembered nothing of her dream, but she was left with a very strange sensation, as if a door in her brain had opened just a crack sometime in the night while she slept. A little dim bit of light seemed to sweep through her head. The cabin was very still but she sensed that Moira was awake. "You awake, Mo?" she whispered.

"Yeah, I am."

"Have you ever wondered about the names of things? I mean why they call something something."

"What?"

"I mean, just for example, what does the word 'original' really mean? I know what an Original is, but have you ever wondered what the word itself means—why they call Originals that?"

Moira was quiet for a very long time. "You know, Darci, I never thought I had. I mean if someone had asked me this maybe a month ago, I would have thought, gee, what a nutty question. It is in a way, but I think . . ." She paused. "I think maybe I have thought about this in some way. And I'm not sure when or why or even how. It's almost like this thing, this old ancient thing, is knocking around, kind of muffled in the back of my brain."

Darci sat up in bed, fully awake and totally alert now. Mo had put it perfectly. There was something knocking around way back in her brain—was it from back in time? In space? She didn't know, but it was almost as if she could feel that door opening one fraction of a millimeter wider. If there was that ancient knowledge somewhere in her maybe her life was less predictable than she had thought. Maybe something did matter.

Chapter 13

T HEY HAD BEEN CLIMBING THE Greybeards for three days now, Darci, Davis, Jessica, Don, Piet, Beth, and Dave. It was exhilarating, the most exciting and challenging experience Darci had ever had. These were all lead climbing routes, which meant that instead of the rope coming over the top, set previously by a climber, a leader would start at the base, choosing the route and setting the anchors for the next climber. The leader had to be sure to pick and place the anchors well and in no way to endanger the second climber. It became the second climber's task to belay the leader, or to lock off the leader's rope in case of a fall.

Lead climbers can only protect themselves by placing

the clipping anchors as they ascend. The length of a leader's fall depended on the distance between the anchors and the firmness of an anchor's hold.

Before Darci went to the Greybeards she was given an intensive course climbing lead on Little Whiskers. Like most beginning lead climbers she tended to put her protection anchors close together.

When one led one always had to be thinking, not just about oneself but about the other person, the second climber following. This was where all the trust exercises really became operational. One constantly had to be visualizing where he or she would put the next anchor. Was the rope running clear of sharp edges that might shred it? Where would be the best point from which to belay the second climber? Darci had never concentrated so hard in her life. When she climbed second she was always thinking how clever Dave or Davis or Jessica or Piet or Donald had been in their placement of anchors. It was as if you were always climbing with two people inside—yourself as either the leader or the second and the other person who was either the second or the leader. By the fourth day they had climbed spires and chimneys, overhangs and "open books," or diehedrals, formed by two walls of rock coming together at a sharp, often ninety-degree angle to make an inside corner.

By this fourth day Darci had really begun to enjoy

leading and had dared widen the space a bit between her anchor points, which made for a quicker ascent. They were climbing in an amazing section of the Greybeards called the Daggers, which was a formation of multitiered Palmyra stone overhangs. They were called the Daggers because in aerial photographs they appeared like knives on edge. They were not particularly difficult but they did demand attention in terms of where one placed the anchors for the seconds. The Daggers were a popular place to climb and could be approached from either the north or south side of their base. As they rose they narrowed and one could often, if the wind was down, hear the voices of climbers on the other side.

Darci heard nothing except the clear trill of a canyon wren as she moved up the steep chimney crack. She was the lead climber and was belayed from below by Davis. He had told her that at about 125 feet up she would begin to see the creamy color of the Palmyra sandstone change, just before she came out into the first of the multitiered overhangs. Indeed it had. And now as she left the cool shadows of the chimney slot she entered a dazzling world of the whitest sandstone she had ever seen. Once more she heard the trill of the wren. When she came out from under the top of the first overhang she would fix her anchor points and as the lead would become the belayer for Davis below.

She might have been dimly aware of a shadow or perhaps breathing coming from the far edge of the overhang. In the back of her mind she might have thought that possibly another climber had been coming up from the other side of the base of the Daggers, up through another chimney and then out onto the overhang. But she would never be sure. Her own breathing, her own heartbeat, filled her entire being. She had dynoed the last pitch. She was sweating hard. She could hear everything within her pumping. Sometimes she imagined she could hear her own muscle tissue stretching. Her feet were so high now her knees grazed her face. The crux, the hardest move of the pitch, was coming up. She was caught in a crossfire of shadow and white light, now blasting in from the overhang's edge. There was something vaguely familiar about the splintering white light as it raked across her. She had a sense that she had been here before. But she knew better. She had never in her entire life been anyplace like this. When she came out and over the lip of the overhang in the last move the light would be blinding. She felt so alive. The rock felt so alive, its texture inscribing its stories of erosion, of time, on her fingertips. She could feel the slightest change in the grain. She could smell the rain in the rock from last night's thunderstorm. She could feel a light wind riffle the stiff cowlicks of her hair.

Darci rested several seconds in preparation for the final lunge that would propel her over the top of the overhang. She had called down to Davis to tell him that she had reached this point. There was a perfect double-handed hold just near the edge of the overhang. She had been told about it. She had no trouble reaching it and then she waited another half minute to gather her strength. The signal then went from her brain to her femurs, to her feet. Her legs became a blur against the rock. Dead point! She floated for one nanosecond. She was a bird, she was sky, she was all, she was nothing. A door from her dream blew open and she fluttered through, light as a random leaf lost in a treeless world.

She was through, into the white light spangled with sunspots. Then a shadow. Why was a shadow slicing across her face and torso? She should be in shards of glaring light sharp as swords. She was over the lip, on top of the overhang, scrabbling against the gritty sandstone, flat on her belly in a long, cool shadow. She could feel the huge thump of her heart. The rock seemed to reverberate as if she were no longer on a rock but on top of a drum stretched taut with a skin resonating every pulse and heartbeat for all the world to hear. She looked up into the pool of the shadow. A face looked back. Her own.

Chapter 14

THERE WAS ANOTHER. ANOTHER WHAT? *Just another. Don't ask . . .*

"No!" Vivian breathed the word, softly but emphatically. And the face across from hers, the lips in that face said the same word, formed the same small rosy purse around the simple sound. "No!" she said again and the other lips moved in the same way. The clear light from the eyes dissolved the gray of the shadows, suffused it with an eerie green light. Time stopped for both girls. Their eyes crawled over each other's faces. Their thoughts in these first long moments, seconds that became years were parallel: twin spiral galaxies of freckles, cowlicks, the same ones that popped up at the forehead and swirled counterclockwise. So this is not a mirror image. This is not an image. This is not a reflection. This is me.

They both began to tremble. "Darci!" a voice finally penetrated from below. "Darci! You okay?" With the voice came a hope for calm.

"Uh . . . uh yeah, Davis. I'm fine. Just resting."

"Me too," Davis called back.

"I'll get the top anchor point set."

"No rush. I'm taking a water break."

Darci finally turned back to the other girl. "Who are you?" she asked.

"Are you me?" Vivian replied. "Or am I you?"

In that sliver of a second both girls knew that they faced not just each other, but in fact were face-to-face with the most heinous crime that could be committed in the Bio Union. They were the crime as well as the evidence of the crime. One of them was the umbula of the other. The punishment was death by incineration. Both girls stood up very slowly. They were shaking. Darci noticed that she was a fraction of an inch taller. As if reading her mind Vivian asked, "When were you born?"

"January 10, in the year 25. What about you?"

"December 11, in the year 25."

Vivian closed her eyes. "So I am the umbula." In that moment Darci felt as if her breath had been sucked right out of her. A shudder coursed through each girl.

They stood together but were vast distances apart as their brains rocked with the impact of this knowledge, their thoughts now very separate and distinct. *I am only a copy. I am nothing more than a copy. I own nothing. There is nothing unique within me, not one cell, not one molecule. Look how I have looped the rope through my snap locks—the double clove hitch. No one ever does that, but I just started doing it for no reason, and look, she has done the same . . .*

And Darci looked at this copy of herself and felt the glow of a terrible rage. Its heat seemed to spread through her body, a conflagration about to explode in her brain. *I have been violated. How dare this copy stand before me. Who did this? I feel invaded, taken over. Nothing is mine anymore. I am the real me. She is nothing. This is . . .* But her mind could not complete the thought.

"Darci." It was Davis's voice calling. "You ready yet?" Darci stood in stunned silence.

"Answer him," Vivian barked. "He'll think something's wrong."

Everything was wrong. What could be more wrong? But Darci's mouth moved and a voice uttered some words. "No. Just a minute." Was it her voice or was it Vivian's? "Are you climbing alone?" Darci asked.

"No, there are others, but farther down than your guy," Vivian said.

"We can't be seen together."

"I know. We'll be arrested. We'll be . . ."

"Put to death along with my parents and your birth mother."

"My birth mother is already dead."

Darci blinked. "She is?"

Vivian nodded solemnly.

"Then who takes care of you?" Darci asked.

"My uncle. But . . . but . . ."

"But what?"

"I'm sure he doesn't know."

"How can you be sure?"

"Well, for one thing he keeps talking about some family resemblance to an old grandmother."

"Hah!" Darci laughed acidly. "Fat chance"

"And the other thing . . ." Vivian hesitated.

"What is it?" Darci asked.

"I live on the grounds of the summer palace."

"You *what?*"

"I live on the palace grounds with my uncle. He is the chief gardener."

This was unbelievable. All the palaces of the Prima crawled with security, ranging from the Grenadiers to GENPOL officers. The living proof of the most horrible crime that could be committed in civilization was right under the noses of the Prima's guard and the most elite of the law enforcement officers of the Bio Union!

Darci's mind was working fast now. She crouched over and began securing the belaying ropes into the top anchor points. "Be right with you, Davis."

"No rush. Enjoying the scenery." Both the girls looked at one another and grimaced. Their mouths pulled into identical sour lines and the single thought flashed through their two brains: better the scenery down there than up here.

"Look," said Darci. "We can never see each other again. NEVER! Do you understand that?"

Vivian colored. "Of course I do. You think I'm some sort of an idiot? You think I want to die? Look, just because I'm your umbula doesn't mean I can't think for myself. Kindly don't speak to me in that condescending manner!" Her eyes flashed in that odd way, like the Original's eyes had when Darci had seen them at Malben's with Max.

"I'm never going to speak to you again. You've got to go. Davis is coming up."

"I'll rappel down to the next overhang on the side I came up from. They often stop there for lunch. I'll tell them that we don't want to get to the top because a whole class is expected and it'll be too crowded."

"Good," said Darci.

Vivian made ready to begin her descent. Just as she was about to slip over the edge Darci called to her softly, "What's your name?"

"Vivian. But everyone calls me Viv." She cocked her head and flicked upward with her chin. "What's yours?"

"Darci."

"You know, Darci, it's not our fault. We didn't do anything wrong."

"Yeah, well, that doesn't play with GENPOL and CERA Funny thing about that."

"But it's our parents who are the criminals."

"Yeah, I know. I find that small comfort. Besides, your birth mom is already dead. They can't exactly kill her twice."

Vivian flinched. "I know, but one more thing?"

Oh, jeez, was this creature going to sit around and blab forever? She had to get out now! Now, before they were discovered. "So what is it?"

"You think I'm your copy. You think you have in some way been lessened by my very existence on the same planet. But I'm not just your copy, Darci. I'm more than that." She spoke in that halting rhythm that Originals sometimes fell into in times of stress—as if the words couldn't be grasped quite quickly enough. Gusts of a hot noonday wind had started to blow. The girls looked at each other in a fierce white glare of reflected light.

"Yeah, well, what are you then?"

"I'm not sure, but I know I am ME and that is different from you." She flicked her head once more, then in one fluid and silent move Vivian slipped over the edge and seemed to dissolve into the thin blue air.

Chapter 15

THAT NIGHT DARCI DREAMED OF THE
door in the rock again. And this time there was no
tracing with her fingertips to find its seams. It was perfectly clear. It swung wide open. On the other side
stood Vivian with a mocking smile. *"And you thought
there might be a point to life? It's me. That's why you bothered
being born. Two entire lives completely mapped out. See nothing matters. Nothing is unpredictable in you. Nothing in me.
We are identical."* How dare she smile! Darci fumed in
her dream. How dare she! And then she heard a door
swing shut. It was not the rock door at all. It was the
one in her brain. And it slammed. The noise startled
her.

"Darci! Darci! Wake up." Mo was leaning over, shaking her shoulder.

"What's going on down there?" Peggy mumbled, half asleep.

"Nothing," said Mo.

Darci was suddenly wide awake. She sat straight up in bed and clutched Mo's hand. "What did I say? Did I say anything? What did I say?" She was frantic with a bottomless kind of terror. Had she spoken of her umbula? Had she said anything in her sleep to even slightly suggest that . . . that she was . . . Oh, Otherness! She couldn't finish the thought.

"You didn't say anything, Darci. No words at least. You just kind of yelped."

"Is that all?"

"Yes."

"Are you sure? I just yelped?"

"Yeah, like you were really scared. Like maybe you were dreaming about climbing and you fell."

"Yes," Darci answered quickly. "That's it. Yeah, you know I had to climb some of those overhangs today and even though a lot of anchors have been set and are supposedly checked constantly . . . you know how it is, you always worry. I think I was worrying about that . . . yes, yes, I'm sure I remember now. I could just see those anchor pins loosening in the rock. The sandstone sort of crumbling around them." She was talking fast now. Was

◊ 105 ◊

she talking too fast to be convincing? She was lying about a dream she didn't have. The irony of it was that to the ordinary person this dream would seem a lot scarier than the one with the door, that is if he or she didn't know what was on the other side of the door. The door! She could feel her heart race again. She could hear that door in her brain slam shut.

"Maybe you want a drink of water? I'll get one for you," Mo offered.

"Oh, I'll get it myself." Darci knew it would be good for her to get out of her bunk, out of the cabin, and walk the short distance to the pump. The night was cool. A slight wind blew. Maybe it would clear her mind.

Darci walked down the pine needle path with her tin water cup. Her nightgown trailed out from under her windbreaker. She got to the well and pumped water into the bucket. She was about to dip her cup in when she noticed the pinpoints of sparkling light. A whole piece of the sky was reflected in the bucket. Darci sat down on a stump by the well and peered intently at the stars floating on the dark surface. She moved the bucket slightly. The stars sloshed and then the crescent moon swam onto the surface. The water grew still again and the stars and the moon, silver-bright, were inches from her fingertips. The Milky Way in a bucket! Time, space, suddenly contracted in a new syncopated rhythm. A piece of the universe inches away. But what does it all mean, what does anything mean? she thought as she looked at this quivering fragment of the universe in the bucket.

Vivian had been right when she said that her very existence on the planet in some way lessened Darci. Did it matter? Reflected back at her from the bucket was just a piece of the Milky Way, throngs of stars. Her sixth-grade science teacher had said that if they had filled the their whole school with sand, and each grain of sand counted for a star in the Milky Way galaxy, they would still need more room. And what was the Milky Way, but a small scrap of a universe, a universe of countless galaxies and billions of stars?

Darci dipped her hand into the bucket and for a split second held infinity in her palm. Dead point. Then the burning stars ran through her fingers. Vivian had said she wasn't *just* a copy. She was more. More what? Darci touched her cheek and knew even in the dark that on another cheek an identical spiral of freckles swirled. Where did she end and Vivian begin?

She thought of Edmar Golenc's umbula now safely implanted in a birth mother's womb, no longer an embryo but a fetus—twitching, pulsing, soon to be kicking. But Edmar and his umbula would only share a short time on Earth together. They were separated by so many years. It was not the same. No wonder there were rules and laws about this. Darci felt herself shrinking, becoming nothing. Soon she would be smaller than one of the pinpricks of light in the bucket.

A mockery had been made of what the Bio Union valued most—DNA. False Others had been presented. And Vivian, so stupid, she thought there was more, that she was more than just a copy. But everyone knew that the very essence of being human was threaded through the twisted helical strands of the DNA; therein lay the true identity of a human being. Of course they would burn Vivian and Darci, her parents as well—burn all of them. It was the perfect punishment. For only through incineration could the DNA, which had been violated, be completely destroyed. The punishment fit the crime. How long would it take for them to be found out?

But why had her parents done this? Was it an act of love? Pride? They could have had other children. Juditha and Leon had other embryos frozen. Embryokin #3, the nonathletic mathematician. Sisters and brothers, not umbulas. Why had they never implanted any of those? Why did they have to make a copy? If she had been an Original none of this would have ever happened.

Suddenly, in Darci's mind the Originals had a special grace, a sacredness, a value beyond what she or any Genhant could imagine. She felt this on some deep, unspeakable level. She knew it in a way she had never known anything before in her life. Darci's mind strained, strained to reach back in time. She looked into the bucket again that held a piece of her own galaxy and then she looked up at the sky. Astronomers looked through their powerful telescopes and sent their probes into deep space to find clues to the birth of the universe, artifacts of fossil fire and light, ancient stars from that first explosion, the Big Bang, and now Darci herself felt as if she were some sort of astronomer. She, however, was not looking for starry skeletons from the past but remnants of ancient genes from another time, a time full of wonder, full of grace, when ova and sperm were not guided on their paths in tubes and glass dishes, when electrical impulses were not used to trigger a "fertilization event"—a time of cripples and geniuses, a time of fools and saints, a time of chance and yes, truth—a time of grace and mystery when not all could be controlled and not all was known.

Darci felt her cheeks becoming wet with tears. The stars blurred. She wanted to see Vivian again. She wanted to see her more desperately than she had wanted anything ever in her life.

Chapter 16

On this same night, in a far corner of the summer palace garden, a shadow came out from under the trellis by the gardener's cottage, paused, and looked about. Vivian had not been able to sleep. She had to get out of the cottage, which could be stuffy on summer nights, into the cool air. She had to think. She was afraid that she might wake her uncle, but when she passed his bedroom she did not hear the familiar light snoring and realized he must be out as well. Sometimes he went to friends' houses to play chess. As far as Vivian knew he had no girlfriends. Never had in the entire five years she had lived with him since her mom had died in the car crash. It seemed funny for a man who was as good-looking as her uncle Walter. But he was shy.

Vivian decided to go to the lily pond. It was one of her favorite places. She often went there and waded during the hottest afternoon, when it wasn't a tour day. One could almost swim in the deeper parts. It was a peaceful place where she could think about the entire impossible situation. She existed only as an umbula of someone else. Not a Laureate's umbula, just the umbula of some very ordinary thirteen-year-old girl. Suddenly her entire life seemed meaningless. Oh, Otherness! It was impossible. Inconceivable. But it was a fact.

She had noticed that this . . . this—oh, it was hopeless, what to call her—this Darci creature had a zit just starting on her chin. She supposed that meant in another eleven months she too would have one. How wonderful to have your entire life laid out so completely. She should have asked Darci if she had gotten her period yet. Then she could be prepared. She knew a girl who had gotten it the first time right in the middle of dynoing an overhang. Vivian sat down by the pond's edge and stuck her bare feet in the water. Why was she having all these stupid thoughts about zits and periods, as if that was the only thing she had to think about? She heaved a big sigh that suddenly turned into a small sob. She clamped her hand over her mouth. She didn't want any of the palace guards to find her. They were very nice and never cared what she did, but . . . but that all might change very soon.

What if they were discovered? Palmyra was not a huge city. Yes, there were endless rocks to climb but certain formations were more popular and became magnets to climbers in the region. Maybe she would just have to stop climbing for the rest of the summer. Her uncle always had work for her in the palace gardens. She could make a lot of money that way. She had wanted a bunch of new climbing things—shoes, snap locks, more rope. More rope, but what for, if she wasn't going to climb? Vivian's mind raced. It seemed to be swirling around something, avoiding it. There was something more to think about here. She wasn't focusing. She rested her elbow on her knee and held her forehead. She had to plan her thoughts about this the way she planned her moves on a rock face. *There is a good chance that I might die. Darci might die too. And so will her parents. Not Uncle Walter. He obviously had nothing to do with this. He could not have known that I am an umbula or he would have never taken me in, not right here on the palace grounds.*

Vivian thought some more. Her mother had always told her that she and another Original had married and decided to have a child. They were going to tell the rest of their families of her pregnancy as soon as the diagnostic testing had been completed. Then her father had been killed in a car crash on the day of the diagnostic results. Her mom decided to go ahead with implantation. But now, like a small illumination, something began to glow in her brain: a knowledge seeped in like soft rain. The kids at that camp were all Genhants. There were no scholarships. No Originals. Darci had to be a Genhant. Vivian gasped and whispered softly to herself the astonishing realization that burst in her brain: "I am not an Original. I am a Genhant. I have the forty-eighth chromosome!"

She looked around her. Did the world seem different in some inexplicable way? The white roses on the trellis were still white, pale and luminous in the night. The ornamental grasses edging the pond still quivered with the breeze. The stars still hung in the sky. She tipped her head and watched them. Nothing had changed and yet everything had. Vivian was more than what she thought she was and still at the same time she was less. She was an umbula. There was a small sinking feeling somewhere within her. Something nagged at the back of her brain. Words. Words carried on a hot white wind. *I'm not just your copy, Darci. I'm more than just that . . . I know I am ME and that is different from you.*

Vivian was now trembling so violently that it was hard to imagine that she had said those words so fiercely. And what did it matter anyway? They would both die. They would both be burned up. At least Uncle Walter wouldn't be involved. Poor, shy Uncle Walter— what would he do when he found out?

As Vivian was going back to the cottage she thought

she saw two figures slide across a path of moonlight. Something made her stop in the long, narrow shadow cast by a cypress tree. She stood perfectly still, hardly breathing. The figures slipped out from behind a shrub; they were embracing passionately. Lovers! Probably a Grenadier and one of the Prima's maids. The Grenadiers were notorious flirts. Women fell for them all the time.

When Vivian sank wearily onto her bed, she felt an indescribable heaviness. The forty-eighth chromosome can't weigh that much, she chided herself acidly. She settled under the covers for the rest of a sleepless night. And if she did sleep, would she and Darci dream the same dreams? Oh yes, most likely. She had never seen the Incinerarium but she could imagine it. She could imagine the flames. She could imagine the ashes. . . .

Usually death meant absence where presence had once been. But execution for umbulae and the people responsible for their creation meant more. They burned the people so there would be no genetic material left. Even embryokins in storage were burned. It was a punishment perfectly suited for the crime. It was total destruction. An extinction. It made a nearly complete and perfect vacuum in a family's gen pro.

A vacuum was really a different kind of nothingness than an absence caused by natural death. Something is missing in a vacuum but not in the feeling way, not in the emotional way, just in a mechanical sense. It was a void. And yet, ashes or not, Vivian knew that she was more than the twisting, spiraling threads that packaged those molecules of DNA. The void that her death would make had to be more than just a physiological or mechanical emptiness. Vivian's hands and fingers made flittering motions across the top of the sheets. Her chin sometimes cocked in emphasis. She was in a deep dialogue with herself. Although the words were never spoken aloud they silently made a calligraphy in her brain that was expressed in the quick, muted motions of her body. Vivian knew that she was more than those bases of sugar and purine and adenine and guanine, of cytosine and thymine, of uracil and pyrmidine. The chemical names strung through her mind like some obscene nursery rhyme. They had first sung the "bases song" in the second grade. That was the Originals' introduction to DNA. Genhant second graders went further because in Genhant schools children were already being taught how to use super electron and laser microscopes. But Originals sang songs and learned the information in a rote, mechanical way.

A dark feeling crept through Vivian. If DNA was the basis of life as they had been taught, if all this could be reduced to ashes, if a perfect vacuum could be created when a life was destroyed, then what was the point of life? Vivian felt sure that there was more to life, much more, that in some way made special the individual—

even if that individual was a copy. There had to be something more that made a human human. Perhaps it was something like memory—not quite memory, but something that defined the true self. Chemical bases could not define the true self. Somewhere there must be a word for this true self. She supposed the scientists at the Library of Dead Language might discover it someday. But it didn't matter if they did or did not find this word. Somewhere deep within her Vivian knew this thing, named or nameless, existed and defined her and separated her from her genetic identical, the girl named Darci.

Vivian looked out the window beside her bed. Such a starry night. The sky seemed to tilt with the weight of the stars. One suddenly streaked across the night, then another. Her eyes jangled in her head and within her skull stars and shooting stars blossomed like a celestial city. Vivian knew with a certainty she had never before felt that at this same moment Darci was looking at these same stars. *But we are different*, she whispered to the sky, *we are different.*

Chapter 17

"YOU SEEM DIFFERENT, DARCI," MAX Lasovetch said.

Darci turned from the terminal in the Dead Language lab and glared at him. "You keep saying that. I'm not different. I'm the same, except for my hamstring." She tapped her thigh, which was wrapped with an ace bandage. It was the second time that Darci had visited the lab in a week. The first time she was not really sure why she had come. It had been the day after what she now thought of as THE ENCOUNTER. She thought that she might be too distracted to climb the Greybeards safely. But more important, she just needed to be near Max, even though she knew she couldn't tell him anything. She had so much bottled up inside of her, and there was no way she could write about any of it in the notebook. What if someone found it, or just happened to look over her shoulder while she was writing—like Rena or Peggy, the Quad Queens as she and Moira called them? Oh yeah, she could envision it. There she'd be writing *Gee whiz, met my umbula today. She's cute—well, what else, having been umbellated from me? She doesn't have a zit yet, but she will in eleven months!*

So she thought just being around Max would help. But it hadn't really. He noticed something was different. Couldn't let it go. Like a dog with a bone. Luckily, though, by the end of her first visit she had really gotten into some of the puzzles that the language scientists were trying to figure out in the lab. But it wasn't her interest alone that had brought her back. She had been right about the distraction and the safety factor. Two days after her first visit to Max when she was back on the Greybeards executing a very simple move, nothing like the dyno looping she had done on the overhangs, she had stemmed out with her right leg, straddling around the corner of a chimney. She hadn't been thinking right at all about her body, its orientation on the rock, and where she was stemming out to. In the weight shift, she didn't fall, luckily, but a shooting pain like a hot knife sliced up the back of her thigh. She knew instantly that she had pulled—more like shredded—her hamstring. There was only a week left of camp, but her climbing days were officially over for the summer. Beth and Dave and Arnie seemed to feel much worse about it than Darci. They thought it a fine idea that she visit her friend Max at the Library of Dead Language.

She was helping him now on part of a project that he was doing for his brother. They were working on something called Fragments. It was indeed fragments in every sense of the word—shattered fossil pieces of poetry, songs, and visuals from before the Reproductive Reformation. They had given Darci a fairly easy fragment on which much recovery work had already been done. A 20 percent recovery rate was considered great. And on this particular fragment they were nearing the 30 percent rate from something they called The Book. It had apparently contained religious stories. There was one on which they had made great progress and they gave that one to Darci to fiddle with, mostly as an exercise in getting used to their techniques in setting up the computer analysis programs.

This particular fragment they were calling Project Noah. There had apparently been a near extinction, a flood of some sort, and to save the various species an ancient man, most likely a sea captain called Noah, had loaded a pair of every kind of animal onto a special boat called the Ark. No one knew yet how the story ended. The greatest discovery the language scientists had made was that what people now called The Otherness, long long ago people had called God or the Lord. It was this God that had become so angry that he roared at the earth, "I will destroy man, whom I have created from the face of the earth; both man and beast and creeping thing, and fowl of the air; for it repenteth me that I have made them." In reading the fragments Darci had a very vivid picture of the story, especially of when the animals had entered the Ark. The verse was quite clear: "They went in two by two." Darci pictured them all—dogs, cats, swans, even mice. It was a nice picture.

Max was working mostly with visual materials, old digital tapes and laser disks. Along with his brother and two other scientists they had in fact made great strides toward that 20 percent mark with their work on what they called the "Half of Life vis-aud disk." It was from that disk that they had reconstructed the one phrase, "half of life is showing up," which Max had spat out at Marilyn Hammertz outside school that day just after the Reading of the Lists

Max and his brother and the scientists had endless arguments over this disk. There were two camps. One camp, Max and his brother, Seth, felt that this vis-aud disk had actually been some sort of an artistic endeavor, a drama, possibly even a comedy. The other three scientists thought this was absolutely preposterous. They were convinced that the tape was a record of the first very primitive attempts at umbellation or perhaps a training tape. One thing for sure had come out of their research, which they all agreed upon and would be a breakthrough in terms of language science. They had in fact uncovered a kind of missing link in the language of genetic technology. Umbellation had once been called *cloning* and umbulae had once been referred to as *clones*. The term had been quickly dropped at the end of the twenty-second century.

On one hand this discovery was great, but on the other hand the scientists were still hopelessly confused for it had shed little direct light on what had absorbed language scientists for the last two centuries—the true source of the word umbellation. There had been a period—the Dark Time, they called it—early on during the Reproductive Reformation, when there had been an epidemic and radical reconstruction of the language used for describing technological procedures. The procedures for gene splitting, umbellation, cryogenically freezing embryos and probing them had grown at an exponential rate. Language could hardly keep up. But more important, during this dark period some people wanted to stop the Reformation, to stop all the new technologies. Somehow language began to play a part in this confrontation. Terms were changed, new names given, and old words along with their meanings lost.

When Darci first came to the Library of Dead

Language, Max's brother, Seth, explained his job simply. "We are scientists in the business of recovering meaning. That's our job. If people, if the Bio Union, want to take in the meaning, use it, maybe reinterpret it based on what we have found—that's their decision. We can't tell the people what to do with meaning."

At that moment the senior scientist, Bernie Nogov, had come in. "You can lead a horse to water but you can't make him drink." Darci had never heard the expression before. It seemed very quaint and picturesque. All of these scientists were constantly sprinkling their talk with such vivid word pictures that they had picked up through their years of excavating pre-Reformationist languages.

"Look, Max." Darci's face softened. "I'm no different. I am, I admit, a little out of sorts with my leg. It still hurts." That was a lie but if it helped explain her behavior to people, who cared? "Just let me be. I like working on these fragments. Takes my mind off the pain." Even if the pain part was baloney she really did enjoy the work she was doing. They had the poetry disks divided as best they could into subject matter and she had hit a group of fairly well-preserved poems about nature. Many had 20 percent of their text or more intact. They were, for the most part, short pieces to begin with.

Several fragments now appeared on the screen. Darci

scanned them. Then her eyes like iron filings to a magnet were drawn to one.

> *The smallest star in me*
> *was split in two*
> *for her*
>
> *In the dark couplets,*
> *cathedrals of atoms*
> *in the honeycomb of every cell*
> *and cubed molecule*
> *in the silver of my body. . . .*

A shudder racked Darci's body. She felt her forehead break out in beads of sweat. STAR SPLIT! That's what she and Vivian were.

She had to see Vivian as soon as possible.

Chapter 18

"You changed your hair," Vivian said. "And what happened to your leg?"

"Shredded my hamstring making a really stupid move on that chimney, you know the one before the overhangs on the south side of the Greybeards, and . . ." Darci sighed. "I changed my hair for obvious reasons."

"You look good as a redhead."

"It goes without saying you would too. We've got the complexion. Our mother has red hair." Darci hadn't meant to sound rude but she knew she did. "Look, I'm sorry. This is just all so weird. I'm glad you got my note okay." Darci looked at her hard. Vivian made the flicking motions with her head. It was actually more with her chin than her entire head. And she watched her eyes. This was her umbula but even so Vivian had somehow acquired those distinctive gestures of the Originals.

"Yeah, I did. That must have taken nerve for you to come to the Prima's garden party, find the cottage and all, and leave the note for me."

"Well, that's why I dyed my hair."

"And cut it too," Vivian said.

"You have to get it really short or really long to tame the cowlicks."

"Don't I know it," Vivian said, patting her own hair.

They were meeting in a park halfway between the Library of Dead Language and the summer palace. Darci had purposely picked a spot by a fountain that was very loud. The water noise would be a good camouflage. She did not want anyone to overhear anything they said. But now a long silence stretched between them that was filled only by the roar of the three gushing waterspouts that erupted in the middle of the pool. Finally Vivian broke the silence. "Well, as I said, that took nerve for you to come to that garden party."

"Yeah, I can't say I exactly enjoyed it."

"Did you meet the Prima? I mean, there is usually a receiving line. She's kind of mechanical in the way she greets people, but she manages some small chitchat. It's amazing. She can just pull anything out of the air to blab about for ten seconds or so with anyone. Then her staff moves you on."

"I guess it's a talent that comes with the job, brought to an art, so to speak, over thirty-one previous generations."

"Guess so. Did she say anything special to you?"

"No," Darci said. "But I was kind of, well, not lingering."

"She didn't say anything like . . . like . . ." Vivian groped for the words.

"Like, 'you resemble the chief gardener's niece'?"

They both laughed. "Well, I hope I don't now since I cut my hair and dyed it."

"Did the kids at your camp think it was funny that you did that?"

"No, experimenting with hair coloring is nearly a pastime. A girl in another cabin with really light hair did a black-and-white checkerboard pattern."

"Gee, how did she do that?"

"Look, we're not here to talk about hair," Darci said shortly. Vivian glowered. Otherness, this girl was stuck up! Maybe she should remind her that although she had gone to school with Originals she *was* a Genhant.

A silence seemed to wrap around them. "Maybe this meeting was a bad idea," Darci said, then muttered, "What am I saying? The whole thing is a bad idea from the start. I could just kill my . . ." She broke off the sentence but Vivian knew what she was going to say: "kill my parents."

"Look," Vivian said. "If you hadn't come, I would have somehow come to you."

"Really?"

"Yeah, really," Vivian repeated.

Darci didn't know if she felt good or bad about this. She dug her hand into her jeans pocket. "I brought something for you." It was a small piece of paper.

"What is it?" Vivian asked.

"Read it."

Vivian began reading the fragment that Darci had found in the poetry fragments file.

"Star split." Vivian whispered the words in a low voice.

"It's a fossilized language fragment, an artifact poem."

"But it doesn't seem like a fossil, does it? I mean, it seems so real. It's like . . . you know . . ."

"Us." The two girls spoke the single word at once.

Darci closed her eyes briefly. It has meaning, she thought. This is from a time when words had meaning. Then she remembered what Max's brother, Seth, had said, that it was up to the people, to the Bio Union, as to how they use or take in or reinterpret the meaning. She and Vivian might be split from a single star but they were criminals. They would die because of their very existence. It had not always been this way, she was sure. Maybe way back during the period they called the Dark Time things were much different. Maybe the world had been whole then, and everything sharp with meaning and yet still there would have been mystery and not all would have been known.

But now was not the Dark Time. They were in the time of Grand Illumination. That was how people had referred to the recent centuries. Now people knew what to do with all these technologies; they knew how stupid it was to umbellate super athletes, for that ended competition. They knew how to write the eloquent laws that protected society against its worst instincts for vanities and the frivolous exploitation of genetic engineering. They were living at the golden apex of the Reproductive Reformation. But for Darci and Vivian shadows had begun to slide across this bright golden place. Words were shattering, meaning receding, and even the embryos—those lovely stuck-together concoctions of hopes and dreams—were being torn apart into nightmares and flames.

"Do you ever dream?" Darci asked.

"Sometimes."

"Well, I've been having this one dream and I have never been able to quite remember it when I wake up. But when I saw you, when we met at the Greybeards, I think that this was part of that dream. It all seemed so familiar." Darci stopped and swallowed. "You ever have a dream like that?"

Vivian shook her head. Darci wondered if she were lying. She probably wouldn't want to admit it if she had had such a dream. "It means a lot to you, being different from me, doesn't it?"

"I am different," Vivian said quietly.

"How can you be so sure?" Darci replied

"How can you be so sure that I'm just a copy?"

Darci's eyes opened wide. "Because . . . because." She started again. "Oh, well, what does it matter anyhow? Even if you weren't a copy, even if you didn't exist, I honestly don't know why I was ever born. What does anything matter in a place like this?"

"What in the name of Otherness are you talking about?" Vivian was completely perplexed.

"Vivian, what is the point of life if everything has already been perfectly designed for a person, if everything is completely predictable, if there is never any chance or real risk?"

"You're crazy. Absolutely crazy. We are living proof. I am living proof of the unpredictable." Vivian began speaking rapidly, her hands and head moving in their own dance. "I am a copy of you. I am a Genhant. But I've been raised as an Original. Look at the way I talk. Lots of the words you say I don't even know. You try and use your hands and your head like mine, you'll look like a damn fool. Nothing is stupider-looking than Gen-hant kids trying to act like Originals." Vivian wrinkled her nose with disgust. "They don't look human. They look . . ." She paused, searching for a word, "kind of like toys." Darci blushed as she remembered trying to imitate the kids at Malben's in her bathroom mirror.

"It's conditioning, environmental influences that make you talk that way and give you the gesturing strategies."

"Gesturing strategies!" Vivian spat the words out with contempt.

"No, I swear it is social conditioning."

"So what! It wasn't predicted. I didn't do what I was programmed to do. Don't you get it?"

Darci looked at her. There was something very puzzling here. Meaning kept flitting just out of reach. Vivian could see her struggling. If only Vivian had more words. Her hands and head began a series of quick yet fluid movements, like wind riffling the still water of a pond. In contrast to her body her voice stuttered and stammered. The words seemed to rip from her throat in jagged chunks. "There's this thing. It's . . . it's kind of . . . like memory. But not quite. It makes . . . each of us a true . . . a true and a separate human. It's inside us. But it's not like the . . . the song."

"What song?"

"The bases song we sang in second grade."

"Oh yeah, we sang that in preschool."

"This has . . . nothing . . . to do with DNA."

"But DNA is memory. It is the memory of all we in-herit," Darci said.

"No, it isn't!" This time the words flew out from Vivian like red-hot coals, so fiercely that Darci caught her breath.

"What are you talking about?" Darci felt a tremor rising within her. She felt as if a dam were about to burst.

"I am talking about something . . . within each human being . . . that makes us . . . an individual. It gives us . . . a true . . . self." Vivian spoke with an excruciating slowness. It was as if she were pulling each word from some unimaginable abyss within her. Her hand movements had become more faint. Some pulse seemed to be dimming inside her. But Darci had to hear what this thing was.

"I don't know . . . the word for it. I don't know . . . if there is . . . a word for it . . . or ever was. I'm so . . . sorry."

Darci was overwhelmed by what Vivian had said. She could not help but think that all this time she, Darci, had been obsessed merely by the meanings of words, but Vivian had stretched her mind beyond words and sought a meaning for individual life, for which there might not be or ever have been a word. It seemed like a much more daring venture. And if what Vivian said was true, then even though Darci might be facing death she felt strangely free in a way she had never known.

They were quiet for a long time. "You know," Darci said slowly. "You know, Vivian, how we learned way back in the fourth or fifth grade in beginning cell biology, or you might have learned it in Cultural History."

Vivian had recovered. Her speech seemed more natural. "I might not have learned it, Darci. Remember, I am supposedly an Original. I went to Original schools. They limit our curriculum. I guess so we won't know what we're missing."

Darci supposed that was why Vivian had had so much trouble speaking a few minutes before. It was not an inherent thing that she could not speak fluently. It was due more to social conditioning. She had been around Originals, kids and adults who seemed to lose the grasp of language in stressful situations. They relied on gestures more than words. Their hands and fingers and flicks of their heads seemed to begin where language left off except earlier, for a moment, even gesture seemed to have escaped Vivian.

"Well, this isn't that hard. One of the first big things that happened, a landmark event in the very beginning of the Reformation, was when reprogeneticists could take a single cell, an adult cell, and still it, make it go quiet. They call this the quiescent phase. They did it by starving the cell, cutting back on the nutrients. And when this happened, well, it made possible the impossible. Because at this stage the cells were in an odd phase; they were ready for anything—any directions, any program. The cell might have started out as a saliva cell or a blood cell. But now it could forget its, well, I guess you'd say destiny, and be reprogrammed. The cells were ready to receive new signals that could command them to make another complete human being or maybe just grow some more nerve cells for a spinal-cord injury patient."

"My uncle's friend works as a secretary at the spinal nerve cell farm down in the valley."

"Well, it's the quiescent stage, the stilling that makes it all possible. Now, doesn't it seem odd that for centuries biogeneticists and cell biologists had been able to reprogram genes to express whatever they want and yet now we live—"

"In a world that makes no sense," Vivian blurted out.

"Exactly! If a cell can be reprogrammed why can't the whole world, or at least the Bio Union, be reprogrammed?"

"Maybe we need a quiescent period." Vivian said.

The words had a powerful effect on Darci. "Maybe this is the quiescent period. Maybe this is not the golden era, the Grand Illumination, but the Dark Time in disguise. Maybe we're really starving. Everything changed after the Dark Time. Changed for the worse, I think, but maybe . . ."

"It's all maybes, Darci," Vivian said. She stood up. "What is definitely not maybe is good-bye."

Darci stood up now too. "It's forever."

Vivian dipped her chin in a barely perceptible nod of agreement.

Each girl turned and began to walk in opposite directions. They had walked no more than twenty-five paces when they both turned and looked at one another.

Star split, Darci thought, but in that moment she realized that her existence had not been lessened on this planet by Vivian; that Vivian was more than just a copy.

And Vivian looked at Darci and thought of that split star from a time before time.

I am ME, she thought. We are two different parts of a single star but I am myself, different, separate, unique, and you are yourself. And neither of us should die.

Chapter 19

"It's more than just the red hair. You seem subdued since you've been home," Juditha Murlowe said and reached over, patting Darci's hand. Of course she was subdued. All Darci could think of was the three of them and Vivian standing in front of the immense doors of the Incinerarium. She would never know if it was the mere touch of her mother's hand that broke her, but suddenly tears started streaming down her face.

"Why did you do it? Why? How could you have?"

It was as if the air had been sucked from the room. The shaft of sunlight that fell on the breakfast table seemed to shatter soundlessly and the family was seized with the awfulness of the knowledge they shared.

"Mom, Dad, I met her." Darci paused. "I met my umbula."

"It's impossible," Her father gasped. But Darci could tell that they both knew she spoke the truth; they both believed her.

"Why?" Darci whispered. "Why? Why would you ever do such a thing? It's a crime. We could all die."

Her father's face contorted. "That is exactly what is happening now. *All* of us, what we call the humankind, are going to die." Leon's words came in a low hot rasp.

"What? What are you talking about?" Darci asked. Leon and Juditha looked at each other. Darci saw the ghost of a nod pass between them.

Juditha began. "It's really important, Darci, that you understand that we did not just do this for vanity, for pride, for all the hundreds of reasons that are really wrong to do this." Her mother took a deep breath. "Darci, there are others like you out there."

"You mean there are more umbulae of me, for Otherness sake? You mean I'm going to run into these other Darcis every time I turn a corner? Oh, Other! We might as well all go and jump in the Incinerarium right this minute."

"No!" her father said emphatically. "There is only one umbula of you. But there are many other individuals like you."

"What are you talking about?" Darci was totally confused.

"Darci," her mother said, "you are a chimera."

"A what?" Her mother might as well have said "You are a chandelier." "What the heck is a chimera?"

Juditha looked over at Leon. "You'd better explain this."

"The technology of chimerization has been around for a very long time. It is one of the basic steps of embryonic recombination. *Chimera* on one level means a simple combination of different cells from different fertilized eggs. Complete chimeras often have the recombination of genetic material from more than two parents. Or say a same-sex couple wanted to have a child—two women could combine their genetic material within the ova of one. An electrical charge would be given in the same way as with umbellation, fertilization would begin, and two women would have a baby with both of their genes. Two men could also do this. They could combine their genetic material in a donor-provided ova. But in any of these cases it would be immediately apparent through embryonic diagnosis that the child to be born was a chimera. Now, a few of my colleagues and I had been working for a long time on something called 'masked chimeras.' In other words, you could not tell if a baby was a chimera or not."

"Why mask it?" Darci asked.

"Well, that is the other part of the question really, why what we know as humankind is going to die out.

The technology of genetic enhancement has given us all so many wonderful things, but recently a few people began to question this. These questions weren't especially welcomed because as you know, for the most part genetic enhancement technologies are in the hands of private industry. It's big business—billions and billions in terms of money. If the government starts saying 'no you can't do this,' well, folks are going to start yelling about free enterprise, and of course a lot of scientists will be out of work, including me. But then your mom and her colleagues at BOG came up with something really scary—a mathematical model that virtually spelled—well, if not extinction, a kind of breaking up of humankind, ironically, for the Genhants and not for the Originals. Although ultimately it would probably include them as well.

"The point is that we are seeing what mathematicians are calling a 'great fracturing,' a breaking up amongst the Genhants. Several genetic enhancement companies are now making great progress in developing the forty-ninth and fiftieth chromosomes. That means more material can be packed on. Okay, so we know we cannot pack on for Vanities, but there still is plenty of room for variation within the range of attributes that can be designed into a new chromosone. We saw this with the forty-eighth—one company favors one kind of genetic modification—maybe they deal with Zolnotz exclusively. We went to a company that specialized in Zol-notz. Another company is known for its manipulations of genetic material that has to do with the musically gifted. People's tastes vary. They choose one firm over another. We are beginning to see divergences within Genhants that show us to be on course for dividing into three entirely separate species. Remember, it didn't take that long for birds millions of years ago to diverge into parakeets, finches, ducks, robins, and the thousands of different species. But in this case, where we are actually planning these genetic alterations, it will happen much more quickly, more dramatically, and we shall eventually lose what we call humankind."

"But there are always the Bio Rads," Darci whispered. She had never been quite sure what a Bio Rad was, but she knew it had something to do with marrying "outside."

"Yes," said Leon. "But the Bio Radicals are virtually cut off from society. They are socially, economically, and politically more disadvantaged than Originals. But indeed, this whole thing began with the Bio Rads."

Darci was getting impatient. "What do you mean, 'this whole thing'? This is about *me*, me and Vivian." Her parents eyes seemed to go blank for a split second.

"Vivian." Darci spit out the name. "You didn't even know her name, did you?" She felt a fury growing inside her.

"No . . . no, no, baby." Her father patted her cheek. Darci jerked her head away.

"Okay, let's get back to me. I am a chimera, which at this point doesn't sound all that different or weird except that there is this other chimera out there named Vivian."

"All right," Leon continued. "Darci, there are a lot of people like your mom and me who can see where we are going with genetic enhancement—the Great Fracturing—and we hope to prevent it through masking. Masking is an attempt to covertly reintroduce Original genetic material back into the entire gene pool. Your mom and I are part of an underground movement to try and do this."

A sick feeling began to swim up in Darci's stomach. There was something sweet and warm in the back of her throat. She might vomit any second. She swallowed and felt her forehead break out in sweat. "You mean I am an Original?"

"Not exactly."

"What do you mean, 'not exactly'?" Suddenly Darci was so sick of words never meaning what they were supposed to.

"Don't worry, you have the forty-eighth chromosome," her mother said quickly. "But you also have some masked genetic material from an Original."

"Vivian's birth mother."

"No, no. Someone else."

"But what about Vivian? I still don't get it. Why after all the masking did you go and do this crazy thing and umbellate me?"

"We thought you were going to die, sweetie. When you were barely six weeks old you came down with stronichylimia. We couldn't afford to lose one masked chimera. You have no idea how quickly we are racing toward the breaking up."

"But what about the other embryos you have frozen? You could have always used one of them."

"No. The masking didn't work in them. We'd just begun to do it. It was only working in less than two percent of the attempts. When you got sick, well, they were collecting blood and marrow from all the sick stronichylimia babies for development of a vaccine. It was just so easy to, you know, get some cells for . . ."

"For Vivian," Darci said quietly. She looked up slowly. "You said there were others." Her parents nodded. "Do any of them have umbulae?"

"We wouldn't know."

"Are there a lot of these masked chimera walking around though?"

"A fair number, because the numbers in the underground have grown. Most of the chimeras are offspring of these people."

"Anyone I know?"

"Max Lasovetch."

"Max! Does he know?"

Her parents both shook their heads. "There's no sense in telling."

Moira! Darci suddenly thought. Could she be one? She remembered that night when Moira had been reading—the fluttering hands, like a bird in flight. And yet if this nimbleness with gesture rather than with language was a learned thing, a part of one's social conditioning as she had thought with Vivian the second time they had met, how was it possible for Moira, who had been raised and educated as a Genhant, to have such skills? And why then did she, Darci, look like a fool when she had tried that time to imitate the Originals' flicking motions and hand movements in the mirror? What was learned and what was forever inscribed in her genes? How did one ever sort it out? She nearly laughed at the irony of her wonder, for indeed wasn't that just the point of the Reproductive Reformation— they thought they had it *all* sorted out.

Darci sighed. She ran her fingers across her head and remembered too late that she didn't even have the solace of longer hair. Her fingers just scraped against her skull. "How did you decide on Vivian's birth mother?"

"We didn't," said Leon. "They try to separate the genetic parents from the birth parents as much as possible throughout the entire process. Someone else handles it."

"But how," Juditha finally blurted out, "did the two of you ever cross paths? We would have never allowed you to go to that camp if we thought she was there. We thought this Vivian . . ."

"Don't call her 'this Vivian'! She is a real person. She is not just a copy." Darci's words startled her. So she had finally said it. She wondered how long she had really known it, known it deep in her gut. Was it when Vivian had first told her, first slipped over the side of the overhang? Had she seen something, some spark in the same green eyes that just made her realize on some very deep level that here was an entirely separate individual despite all the similarities?

"You're right, dear. But we thought she and her birth mother lived out in the Western Territory of the Federation Lands."

"Well, her mother got killed in a car accident. So she lives with her uncle. And her uncle just happens to be the chief gardener at the summer palace of the Prima."

"Oh, Otherness!" Darci's parents said at once.

Chapter 20

Vivian had tried not to think about Darci, especially about that last good-bye. But it was virtually impossible. The knowledge seeped through her like a slow, inexorably rising tide. Sometimes it just filled her completely. She felt as if she were drowning, and a terrible panic would grip her. If she had someone she could talk to about this it would help, but there was no one. Her uncle, never talkative, seemed in these last days of summer more remote, distracted or preoccupied. She had tried to keep herself busy by helping him in the gardens. There was always much to be done at the end of the summer. The pools had to be cleaned, the water lilies taken to the winter greenhouses, the goldfish netted and taken to indoor tanks. Autumn mulch had to be spread. All of the garden tools were meticulously cleaned and oiled. There were hundreds of tasks. School would not be starting for another two weeks. Vivian wondered if now that she knew she was a Genhant she would feel smarter, do better. Her teachers were always saying attitude counted as much as anything. But even with the forty-eighth chromosome, how could this attitude work for her if she was scared to death most of the time?

She had gone rock climbing only once since meeting Darci. It was after the camp ended and she was sure that she would not encounter anyone from the Arc of the Winds camp who would mistake her for Darci. Almost unconsciously she found herself at the base on the north side of the Greybeards. It was as if a taut wire drew her straight up through the chimneys and the slots. Then she looped in a flash of dyno lunges under the overhangs and over the top where she and Darci had first met. She had kept her eyes straight down on the rock as she clambered over the top. She lay on her belly for several minutes before she dared raise her eyes and when she finally did there was no one there. The rock was bare. Clouds scudded across the sky. The world seemed incredibly empty. For a brief few seconds she thought about dying. She thought how a straight, clean fall to the base five hundred feet below would be so much better. She had started to cry softly at first, then she tipped back her head and howled at the sun.

That had been just two days before. Now she followed her uncle Walter around the pond. They both wore thigh-high waders as he dipped down and retrieved the water lilies, plopping them into the basket that Vivian carried. There was to be a reception that night, an elaborate garden dinner and dance. The water-lily baskets would be filled with night-blooming fragrant plants. Other gardeners were installing the plants as Vivian and her uncle scooped up the lilies. They spoke only the few words necessary to do the work. Vivian looked at him while he bent down. He was shirtless so as not to get his clothes wet. He had long, muscular tan arms.

"You've got some pondweed on your beard," Vivian said.

He laughed. It was more of a bark than a real laugh or chuckle. "Guess I better trim it." His beard, just like his hair, was very black and Vivian noticed a few gray streaks. She wasn't sure how old her uncle Walter was, but it suddenly struck her as funny that he had never married.

"Uncle Walter," she finally said as they were walking back to the winter greenhouses with the baskets of water lilies. "How come you never got married?"

"What a question!" His sharp blue eyes opened wide with surprise.

"What do you mean 'what a question'? It's a perfectly reasonable question. You're very good-looking, you know."

"Oh, I am, am I?" Now his eyes twinkled and he smiled. Vivian thought he looked great when he smiled. He had deep dimples—the long kind, not the pit kind. They made his face look lively and friendly.

"You would have had very handsome children," Vivian said. At that moment all the lively blueness seemed to vanish from his eyes. "I'm sorry," Vivian said quickly. "It's none of my business. I'm a busybody, aren't I?"

Uncle Walter set down his basket. "No, you're not, Viv. It's a fair question. I just don't have an answer. To tell you the truth, I've been a bit worried about you lately."

"Me?" A coldness gripped her chest. "Why me?"

"Not sure, dear. You just seem . . . I don't know . . ." He fluttered his hand at some word that slipped through the air like a butterfly. "A bit nervous. A bit . . . a bit frightened."

Vivian didn't know what to say. She could feel the color draining from her face. She could sense the freckles, those twin galaxies standing out on her cheeks, naked, exposed. She had never thought her uncle paid her that much attention. She smiled a quick, bright, and very false smile. "Well, nothing's bothering me. Maybe I'm a little bit nervous about school. You know they say eighth grade is a lot harder than seventh. Just that kind of stuff."

Uncle Walter bent over and picked up his basket again. "Sure, dear. That's probably it. I think I remember being nervous about eighth grade myself." But Vivian knew this was a lie. She knew that he was trying to make her feel better. But of course Uncle Walter wasn't the only liar. The air itself was thick with lies between them. She felt this with an absolute certainly. Yes, he had lied to her about believing her lie about eighth grade, but at the same time he had lied to her too about not having an answer for why he had never married. And he had been lying to her all summer in a way, about where he went in the evenings. Oh, she knew he went out to play chess with friend, or to horticultural meetings. He would come back, make a big show of yawning and going to bed. But ever since that first night, after Vivian had met Darci and had gone to think by the lily pond, she knew her uncle had been leaving very late in the evening and then returning shortly before dawn. He was very quiet, but Vivian had spent so many sleepless nights that she would hear footsteps going down the hall late at night and the creak of the front door of their little cottage. She might sleep fitfully until dawn, then a click, or just the soft thud of a footstep would awaken her and she knew it was her uncle returning from wherever he had been.

The party that evening had been beautiful. The gardens had looked lovely strung with paper lanterns and profusions of flowers and even flower sculptures throughout. The Prima had been very pleased. Her uncle had tried very hard because he knew that this last summer party was always of particular importance to the Prima and the Prima Matri. Her uncle had let Vivian climb what she called her watching tree. It was a good place to observe the fancy outdoor palace parties. There had been wonderful food, and the chefs had sent over a sampling for her and her uncle's own dinner. The women had all worn spectacular dresses. The Prima, however, looked the most beautiful in a shimmering gown of palest pink with embroidered sprays of tiny pearls. The dress was close-fitting. This would be her last public appearance in such a close-fitting gown, for as all thirty-one Primas before her, she was scheduled for implantation of her umbula in late September and would be pregnant throughout the fall and winter and into spring. The thirty-third Prima would arrive precisely on June 24 of the next year, sometime between the hours of six A.M. and noon. The Prima glided through the throngs of people, greeting them all warmly. When the band struck up she danced with several of the men. Then finally, she took her seat on a chair near the lily pond, which now in place of the lilies had floating baskets of flowers. She gazed out toward them. Vivian had a perfect view.

It suddenly struck Vivian that the Prima, who always seemed somewhat removed emotionally from everything, appeared different tonight. She was tinged with a kind of ineffable sadness and as she watched the floating basket of flowers. Vivian thought for one moment that the Prima might even lose her famous composure. She could have sworn she saw a tremor course through the Prima's body. This was so unlike her. Neither the Prima nor the Prima Matri were ever really gay or sad. They were calm. They possessed the eternal calmness of a lake on a windless winter day just on the brink of freezing. *Stillness* was the word that people most thought of when describing the Prima. And it was this stillness that the citizens of the Bio Union found most comforting in their Prima. This Prima, however, despite her outside appearance of calm, was anything but still, Vivian suddenly realized. Oh, she had quelled the little shudder, the tremor that could have passed for a shiver given the bareness of her dress, but there was something troubling the Prima very deeply.

Soon the fireworks started exploding. The star bursts of dazzling lights reminded Vivian of the sprays of pearls on the Prima's dress. She noticed that the Prima Matri had come to sit beside the Prima and that they held each other's hands, and their heads, with blonde and silvery hair like caps of moonlight, touched lightly as they tipped them toward the jeweled sky.

Vivian had gone to bed long before the end of the party. The noise of the music that had washed over her as she lay in her bed on the brink between waking and sleep had long since vanished. The guests from the reception had left hours before. Everything on the palace grounds was still. Now the creak of the door ripped the fragile fabric that Vivian had come to call sleep. She knew it was her uncle going out once again into the night. It took her only a fraction of a second to decide to follow him, although she wasn't sure why. She did not bother with shoes or even a sweater. She would not bother with the door either. The window by her bed was open. She slipped out and waited behind a shrub from which she could see the front door. To her surprise her uncle did not turn left, which would have taken him out the service gates of the palace, but right. To the right led nowhere except into the most remote parts of the garden, to the region called the sylvan, a wooded area. As soon as he was a good ways down the path, Vivian began to follow.

She could not imagine why her uncle was going down to the sylvan. It was certainly not the most comfortable place to be, mosquito-ridden and sometimes in the hottest days of summer filled with a rank sulfurous odor. They did use parts of the sylvan for orchid experimentation. The environment was good for the orchids, which required warmth and high humidity. Vivian was fleet and light. Indeed her Uncle Walter sounded like a charging beast compared to her. She was grateful for the noise he made. It camouflaged any she might make.

At an immense tree hung with moss he stopped. He seemed to dissolve through the thick curtains of the moss. Vivian thought she saw another figure as he parted the curtains. She heard two whispered voices. Then nothing except gasps. She edged down the path. Her eyes had grown accustomed to the darkness. She saw a narrower path, barely a path really, by which she might circle behind the tree and be able to see more. She followed it. The huge old tree seemed completely shrouded in mosses, but here was another tree nearby with some low limbs. If she could climb high enough perhaps it would be like a watching tree.

Smudged moonlight hung dimly in the sylvan. Only as thinner clouds scudded over did a clear silver shaft of light fall into the thick woods. Silently Vivian climbed through the tangle of branches and night shadows. Soon she was high up. She looked down. The moss tree's huge roots twisted and writhed over the forest floor. It took her a minute or more to separate them from the roots, to realize that the two bodies entwined, embracing, kissing passionately were not part of the tree. She saw the familiar fleck of silvery gray in the black hair and then a sudden wind scraped the clouds from the moon and Vivian saw the bright glint of pearls!

She froze. Time stopped. Vivian was not sure if she had been there minutes or hours. When she finally got down from the tree they were gone. The next morning at the breakfast table her uncle Walter seemed the same as always. Perfectly normal. Too normal! Vivian pretended to have a headache and went back to bed without eating. She stayed in bed all morning. She had to think. The meaning of this was overwhelming. When she found out about Darci she had figured they could not blame her uncle, that he would be spared. But this was mind-boggling. The Prima and her uncle Walter were lovers! All Primas for thirty-one generations had been virgins. They had neither lovers nor husbands. They were given a medication from puberty on to suppress their desires. This was unimaginable. Yet she had seen it. This was unthinkable. Yet it had happened.

By noon she had convinced herself that this possibly hadn't happened. That perhaps she had been dreaming or sleepwalking, but then she noticed how dirty the bottoms of her feet were. She decide to get up and walk down to the sylvan, to go back to the moss-hung tree.

She hesitated as she approached the tree. She was standing right where her uncle Walter had stood when he separated the moss curtains. She was afraid. Maybe they were there now, but even worse, she felt as if she were violating some secret private place. She reached out her hand and pushed lightly against the moss. The trunk of the old tree was a soft silvery gray. Shadows swelled under its branches. It was like a lovely cave. She noticed a bright green, furry moss that crept over many of roots. She had not seen this the night before. It seemed like a place of infinite quiet and softness. She walked in. It was cool and nothing stirred. There were two immense roots that splayed out from the base. There was a shallow depression between them that was thick with moss and sprigged with tiny white flowers. Vivian stooped down to run her hand across it. Scattered amid the hairlike filaments of moss were hundreds of tiny white pearls.

Chapter 21

THE BLINK WOUND DOWN THROUGH
the Kerals. The deep folds of the white stone curtains
hung as if from a pure blue sky. The other passengers on
the train oohed and aahed. All of them had seen the
sight before but it never failed to overwhelm even the
most jaded tourist, except for Max Lasovetch, who was
not jaded but merely stunned. For the past eighteen
hours he had hung in a state of disbelief and now horror. The face kept coming back to him. Darci's face, but
of course it wasn't Darci. It was—Max's brain seemed
to nearly spasm. It was as if he could not even think of
the word. It was her umbula.

Yes, now it all made sense. Darci's strange behavior

at the end of camp. And then of course her hair, changing the color, cutting it. Always going around in a baseball cap and sunglasses. He felt a silent sob the size of a tidal wave swell in him. Poor Darci! He tried to imagine how she had felt. It had been bad enough for him when he had rounded that corner. He was just thankful he had been alone. He could have been so easily with his brother or some of the other guys who worked at the lab. On his last night in Palmyra he had a sudden craving for a Keral Kreme, a spectacular creation that cost an arm and a leg and had nearly a quart of ice cream in it. It would be, after all, the last time until next summer that he could indulge in such a spectacular eating experience. Keral Kremes were virtually small mountain ranges of ice cream. You could also order the Palmyra Sandstone Cliff Bonanza or one called The Chocolate Beards. He had just finished eating the entire dish, something few people accomplished. He had cut down a back alley behind the Keral Ice Cream Works. Just as he came out and turned right, in the yellow cone of brightness from the streetlamp there she was. "Darci!" he called out. The girl froze, like an animal caught in headlights. Her feet would not move. It was one, maybe two long awful minutes. Max stood gaping in front of her. Now in retrospect he could remember it all so clearly. There were the first confusing seconds. A voice in his brain saying *This does not make sense. Darci left camp a week ago. Darci left with short red hair.* Then a shattering in his brain. *This is not Darci. This is an umbula of Darci.* It was then that the girl who was not Darci, the umbula, ran. He had never seen anything like it. She didn't just run, she leaped clear over a pedestrian bench in one silent glide, and arcing into the air she was swallowed by the night. He had stood there for several minutes trying to will away what he had just seen. But he knew it was true. It had explained everything about Darci in the last days of her time in the Kerals. He did not know how he would talk to her about it when he got back. But he knew he had to. This was too much for one person alone to live with. There wasn't much he could do, nothing he could do to change things, but maybe he could just be there for her. Then a chill crept through him. Could he really be there for her at the end? He closed his eyes. He would never go on another field trip. He could not bear to see the Incinerarium again.

Vivian lay in bed the next morning. She had not slept all night. She had heard the door creak open when her uncle had left and again toward dawn when he returned. But the relationship between Uncle Walter and the Prima seemed minuscule now in terms of her own problems. She had been spotted. The boy had called out. The name sliced through the night like a bullet.

She felt as if she had been shot. So now at least three people, not including Darci's parents, knew. It could only be a matter of time before . . . before what? She wondered if she should tell her uncle. The little stone cottage covered with ivy, which she had always loved, now seemed like an alien place. Every window, every door, every crack in the walls or ceiling, even the darn chimney seemed like an opening through which people could listen to the secrets and lies that now made up the fabric of her and her uncle's lives.

She might have been raised as an Original but it didn't take that much brain power to realize that although this was a democracy there was one unforgivable crime, and the entire system of laws and law enforcement was organized to prevent that crime from happening and if it did, to make sure the punishment was swift and terrible. There was CERA, the Central Endowment Regulatory Agency, and GENPOL, the Agency for Genetic Policing, who were known as the most brutal of any of the law enforcement divisions. GENPOL was the one branch of the law that, although not exactly above the law of the land, was somewhat to the side of it. It was well known that they were tacitly authorized to use torture in order to obtain information where the laws of reprogenetics and umbellation were suspected to have been violated.

The boy had seen her. It was really only a matter of

time. All this time a thought had been niggling some-where in the very back of Vivian's mind. It was like a fuzzy picture that she could not quite bring into focus or maybe an equation that was not exactly balancing out, but then suddenly it did: If Uncle Walter and the Prima are lovers then they are in as much trouble as Darci and I. One word burst like the brightest firecrack-ers in Vivian's brain. OUTLAWS! "We are all outlaws," Vivian whispered to herself. She knew what she must do. Blades of sunlight lay across her sheets. It was late in the morning. She must get up. She must find her uncle and she must tell him—tell him everything.

Twenty minutes later Vivian sat across from her uncle Walter at the simple wooden table at which they had eaten countless meals. Even though it was a warm day she had closed all the windows.

"Now what is this, Viv dear?" her uncle asked. "I've been really worried about you these last few weeks."

Vivian looked down and did not say anything. She dug her hand into her jeans pocket and pulled out a small piece of cloth that had been tied with a string. She lay it on the table. Her uncle watched her at first with detachment but when she had loosened the strings and unfolded the cloth scores of small pearls rolled across the surface of the table.

They looked at each other. There was nothing

accusatory in her uncle's eyes. They were simply incredibly sad. "So you know." He spoke quietly.

Vivian nodded. "I know."

"And—" Her uncle's voice broke. "Oh, Viv, it's not of your concern."

"It wouldn't be ordinarily," Vivian whispered. Her uncle leaned forward with new attention.

"What do you mean?" he asked. His eyes seemed to dart nervously.

"Uncle Walter, we are all outlaws."

"What do you mean, 'all'?"

"I mean you, the Prima, me, and . . . and Darci."

"Darci? Who is Darci."

"Uncle Walter, I am the umbula of a girl named Darci." Her uncle's face turned white, whiter than the silver in his beard.

"What? That is impossible. Your mother was my sister. She and her husband, they had just gotten married but were anxious for children. They did the embryo . . ."

"It was a lie, Uncle Walter. She lied to you. She lied to me. I know. I have a scrapbook filled with pictures of this man who supposedly was my father. But my genetic father and my genetic mother live in the capital city and they have a daughter named Darci. She is eleven months older than me. The umbellation was started when she was less than two months old."

Her uncle was holding his chin in his hand so that

the palm covered his mouth. His eyes were closed and he was shaking his head back and forth. It was as if every molecule in his being was trying to deny this awful knowledge. Finally he took away his hand and looked around the small modest cottage. Vivian knew what he was thinking. It had been the same for her. One instant their lives had been so normal, perfect, although they would perhaps not have said that at the time, but in comparison, yes, their lives had been perfect, but within the course of one minute everything had changed. This knowledge invaded every corner of the cottage, every seam and crack. It permeated the wood fibers, the curtains. The dust motes turning slowing in the shafts of sunlight swirled to the rhythms of this awful knowledge.

"How did you ever meet her?"

"At the Greybeards." Vivian told him the story. Then she told him about meeting the boy on the street the night before.

"Last night, just last night you saw him?"

Vivian nodded. "What are we going to do, Uncle?" She began to cry.

He got up and folded her in his arms. "This was bound to happen sooner or later." Vivian backed away.

"What do you mean? I don't understand."

"I think, Vivian, that you and I, and my beloved Lana—"

"Lana? Who's Lana?"

"Lana is the Prima."

"But the Prima never has a name, never in over one thousand years has a prima ever had a name."

"This one does. She has named herself. And her name is Lana. And I think that you and Lana and Darci and I are a part of something much bigger. It is coming sooner than we thought. I never imagined that it would touch you quite so directly, but it was bound to happen."

"I still don't understand."

"I know, dear. That is why we must go to the Prima, to Lana."

Chapter 22

Vivian and her uncle had just been brought into the Presence Chamber of the Prima. A life-size portrait of the twenty-second Prima who had presided over the Congress of the Reproductive Statutes and established the Board of Selection, two landmark events in Reproductive Reformation history, hung on the wall behind the Prima's chair. The Prima pushed a button in the arm of the chair she was sitting in. A piece of the wall panel opened, exposing a passageway. The Prima rose and motioned for them to follow. They went down a twisting staircase. They were going to the innermost office of the Prima's private apartments. It seemed far underground. They walked down a short, very narrow corridor and the Prima pushed another button. The door slid open. Just before they entered the Prima turned and said, "Here we can be assured of utmost privacy. The staff knows of this room's existence. They know not ever to interrupt. They only become suspicious if I bring the same people here too often, thus your uncle and I could only use this in the beginning."

Vivian had a million questions. When was the beginning? And weren't they afraid of being discovered in the sylvan? Were there other places they met? These questions immediately fled her mind as she stepped into the room.

"Welcome, dear child and Walter." It was the Prima Matri. Vivian was stunned. She seemed older than she looked from a distance. Her eyes faded, her hair white, and her wrinkles were so fine they seemed to fit her closely like a soft sweater. "I know, my dear, you are surprised. They all are surprised. I have not aged as well as some of my predecessors. Perhaps it is The Troubles"

The Prima laughed. "Stella has the gift of understatement."

"Stella?" Vivian said.

"Me!" The Prima Matri raised her hand in a jaunty wave. "I named myself too. I couldn't stand being nameless. We value words and names so little in this civilization. It was Lana's idea first that we take names. It seemed something like a miracle to have names, and even if we could only use them in secret, it still does. We are just copies, genetic copies, copies of that first Prima over one thousand years ago, but when Lana and I chose our secret names suddenly it gave us a tinge of unique-ness. I felt as if I had added an ounce or two of weight. You know, just slightly more substantial." She waved her hand dismissively. "But I am gabbling on. I know there is much that Lana must tell you, and my dear, we have heard of your terrible plight. Your uncle told us . . ." She shook her head.

"Please sit down." Lana gestured to three upholstered armchairs. "Vivian, you are frightened and rightly so. Your uncle has told me everything and I know that he has told you we believe your fate has intertwined with ours." Lana saw the confusion on Vivian's face. "Yes, I know. It seems strange. Let me try and explain. You see, Vivian, some years ago, oh, before I was twenty, I was approached by a member of an underground movement. The people in this movement were very smart. Many of them were scientists. They had come to realize that this civilization, the Genhants first and foremost, were rush-ing toward a kind of extinction, something they call the Breaking Up or the Great Fracturing." Lana proceeded to explain to Vivian what Darci's parents had told her. Vivian listened carefully.

"We have reason to believe therefore that you might

be one of these masked chimeras. That is the only reason one would risk an unauthorized umbellation of an infant—in order to covertly introduce genetic material of Originals to preserve humankind. Do you understand?"

Vivian nodded. But what she didn't understand was if the entire government was against this, why was the Prima for it? The Prima *was* the government. She was the leader of the Bio Union. How had the underground ever dared come to her? Vivian started to frame her question. "But . . . but what . . ."

Lana broke in. "You want to know why they came to me. How they dared it?"

"Yes. And why would you even believe them?"

She heard Stella laugh. "Something after thirty generations somehow went a little screwy with Lana and me—"

Lana interrupted. "I have to credit Stella. She started the seeds in my mind."

"You're the one who came up with the idea for names, my dear."

"It was just a game at first, but, well, it's like Stella said, suddenly our names seemed to add something to us. Made us more real."

Lana reached out her hand toward Stella. "I call her Stella Nana." Tears were now streaming down the older woman's face. "Something happened between Stella

Nana and me. It was very odd. It had never happened before in the entire history of the Primarchy. You see, if you are a Prima you are never technically a daughter or a mother, you are a copy. Primas are not allowed really to nurture their young umbulae in the ordinary sense. Nurturing is left to nursemaids. What you are asked to be is rather a perfect template; you function as a pattern. Love is not involved. In fact, we are given medications to quiet such passions. But, as I said, something happened between Stella Nana and me. We had both taken the medications for years. The medications were not only supposed to quiet passion, whether it was of a maternal nature or a romantic one, the additional so-called benefit was that of banishing loneliness. That, I suppose, is a blessing. For there is nothing lonelier than the life of a Prima."

"It dulls certain other senses too," added Stella. "For example, we all know that within ten years I shall die. All Primas die within the seventh month of their sixty-ninth year. For most people it would disturb them to know precisely when they will die, but not for Primas—the medications lessen these anxieties."

"But I don't understand," said Vivian. "What happened? Why are you two different? Didn't the medication work?"

"It did up to a point," answered Stella. "But about thirteen or fourteen years ago there was a dreadful virus, stronichylimia, that swept through the Bio Union. They thought at the time that I had just a light case of flu. It was not nearly so bad in older people as it was with young children. But I was left with a slight weakness in my left leg. After that the medications that had usually worked for the Primas seemed to have lessened in their effect. Oh, it was not that I suddenly became this wildly passionate middle-aged woman." Stella laughed and her pale green eyes glinted with light for the first time. "But I felt things—I felt good things and bad things. And one of the things I felt most of all was loneliness."

"Stella, don't let stronichylimia take all the credit. We had invented the names long before that."

"Yes, and I loved the names and I loved them even more after my illness. They seemed to be a gateway out of the loneliness and into something much deeper. I wanted to be a mother, a real mother to Lana, not just a birth mother. It was I who convinced Lana to stop taking the medications. If I were going to mother her, I wanted her to feel it. To know it. We were, after all, starting rather late. Lana was already sixteen."

Lana looked over at Stella, her eyes shimmering with love. "She had always wanted to be a mother—a real mother. That is what I mean when I say that the seeds were always there. Something had changed with us after thousands of years. It's unexplainable on every level, at least that anyone ever talks about in the Bio Union." Vivian could see that Lana had more she wanted to say and was struggling. "This part is difficult to explain. It was not only the medications or rather lack of the medication's, although perhaps that was the trigger for something else to begin to grow within us, aside from the feelings.

"In our society we talk about individuality, we celebrate our Laureates, but do you know the Reading of the Lists and the Endowment Procedure Ceremonies are for me the unhappiest days of the year? These are the days when we actually deny the sanctity of the individual and instead elevate to an Otherness-like position the gene, the chromosome. Oh yes, we can umbellate a great scientist and artist, but you can't copy . . ." Lana paused before saying the next words, "a soul."

"A soul?" Vivian asked. She had never heard the word before. It was such a simple yet lovely sound. It seemed to ring like a distant chime in her mind. "What is a soul?"

"It's a very, very ancient word." Lana spoke quietly.

"A word older than time, I think," Stella added.

Vivian felt something fluttering inside her. Wingbeats in her heart. An excitement grew within her.

"What is a soul?" she asked again.

"The language scientists discovered the word some years ago at the Library of Dead Language, but an immediate decision was made not to publish the research.

It was instantly declared to be classified information, for they sensed even though the research was just in its earliest stages that there was something about this word that was dangerous."

"What could be dangerous?" Vivian had to know, for she felt herself powerfully drawn to this word. Her hands began to flicker in a stuttering motion.

Stella rose from her seat. "My dear, Lana and I are genetically identical. We are identical to every Prima before us for the last one thousand years. I said something went a little screwy but perhaps something, some tiny particle within us, went right and sought something beyond the absolute order that could be dictated by the chemical bases. There were other elements, other powers that could not be reduced to the infinitesimally small bits of DNA that carry the inheritance of, say, a music genius or a great astronomer, or the color of one's eyes or hair. No, this was something else entirely—something beyond the reach of the sugar and proteins, the chemical bases and their intricate linkages. It was these elements, or powers or impulses that drove us to seek names for ourselves. They gave me the instinct for an intimacy with Lana and she with me that was maternal rather than sisterly, for after all we are technically twin sisters even if I did give birth to her."

"Soul." Vivian spoke the word quietly. And the single word was an answer to her own question on the night after she had first met Darci. There would never be a vacuum, could never be one, despite flames, despite ashes, for there was soul. Vivian had been right when she thought that it was something like memory but not quite memory. Memory went back in time and was carried into the future by the next generation, but soul did not know time. It did not know the boundaries of generations or chemical bases, for soul was the true self. Soul was the nameless thing now named that defined and separated her from Darci and every other human being on earth. It was her essence.

Vivian looked at her uncle Walter. He read the question in her eyes. "I fell in love with her soul," he said quietly.

"Are you a part of the underground, Uncle Walter?"

"I wasn't then, but I am now."

"When I met Walter," Lana continued, "I had already been approached by the underground. There are a few people here in the palace who are a part of it. Their ideas both alarmed and interested Stella Nana and me. We had only really been thinking about our own lives, our own loneliness. Now we realized that this insane obsession with DNA, with the forty-eighth chromosome, was literally driving us to the end, a kind of extinction of humankind. We could align our own personal causes with a much more noble one." Lana paused for several seconds. She looked gravely at

Vivian. "The Bio Union must change and to do this the Primarchy must stop. It must end forever," the Prima said quietly.

"But how?"

Lana looked at Walter and then at Stella. They both nodded. "Tell her," Stella said.

"An embryo has been started. It is a masked chimera, like yourself and Darci. It appears to have all of my genetic material. It appears to be the thirty-third Prima but it covertly carries genetic material of an Original. It shall be implanted in my womb in another few weeks."

"Uncle Walter?" Vivian looked at her uncle, her eyes were wide with wonder. Her uncle smiled broadly.

"But how are you ever going to do this?" Vivian asked. "When it's born people will know then, won't they?"

"We will be gone," Uncle Walter said.

"We'll be going to the Western Territory of the Federation Lands, outside the Bio Union. We were going to bring you, Vivian, and Stella too."

"It's just so . . . so amazing."

"I'm going to be a grandmother," Stella said. "A real grandmother." She paused. "But more important, there shall be a new little soul on Earth. A real soul."

"Stella Nana." Lana turned and touched the elder woman's cheek. Their eyes brimmed with tears of a profound, unspeakable love.

Chapter 23

DARCI TOOK A DEEP BREATH BEFORE she walked through the door at Malben's. She was going to do this. She had to do it. The place was crowded. That was what struck her first. So many kids and so little noise. But there was an electricity in the room as they flicked their heads, and their fingers seemed to mold the air around them, punctuating the few words they spoke. Darci gave her order at the counter and slid into a booth to wait for Max Lasovetch. Once more she stared down at the table as if it were the most interesting thing in the world. She would avoid any eye contact. But it was here that she wanted to meet Max, to tell him everything. He knew. He had called her as soon as he came back from the Kerals, and although he would never dare say it over the phone, she knew when he said he needed to see her with that terrible urgency in his voice that he had in fact seen Vivian before he left. Poor Max. She should at least order him a liquid sundae.

She got up again and went to the counter to tell the man to make that two. The counter guy was waiting on someone else. Darci watched. Then he came to her and suddenly it was so easy. She tilted her head with a slight gesture and tapped the air twice with two fingers. The fingers were almost like ditto marks on a paper but the guy knew exactly what she meant. Another liquid sundae. He cut his chin on a slant toward the booth where she was sitting and she understood that he would bring it over to her. Darci felt a sudden flood of happiness. She was communicating without words! She felt as though she had entered a new world. She went back to the booth to wait for Max.

A minute later she looked up and saw him coming through the door. Normally she would have called out a greeting but now she whisked her head quickly from side to side as she had seen the other Originals do when greeting friends. Max looked puzzled. He noticed, thought Darci. He sees how easily I did that. He almost looked disoriented, as if he thought this was Darci but then again maybe it wasn't.

"Darci." The word came out as half question, half

statement, and he paused before sliding into the booth.

"I ordered you a liquid sundae," Darci said as the man came with the tall frosty glasses and set them down. They both sipped silently. Darci liked the silence. She liked this wordless place. From the corner of her eye she could catch the shadows of the Originals' hand gestures against the wall of the booth across the way. "So you met her," she finally said.

"Yeah." Max nodded.

"Are you ready for more?"

"More what?"

Darci in a low voice began to tell him about the Great Fracturing, about the attempt to end an extinction and about the masked chimeras. "And"—she took a deep breath—"you're one, Max."

Max stared in amazement at Darci. It was not that he had grown accustomed to the awful knowledge about Darci and her umbula, but he had not expected any more surprises. He thought all surprises had ended when he had come out of that alley and rounded the corner back in Palmyra.

"I'm a what?" he gasped.

"A masked chimera. Don't worry, you still have the forty-eighth chromosome."

"That's the least of my worries. You mean I've really got some of this Original stuff in me?"

"You bet."

A shadow of a smile stole into the corners of Max's mouth and lighted his eyes. "I think it's like . . . kind of . . . I don't know . . . sort of, well, frankly incredible! Great!"

Darci almost laughed. It was the first time in days she had felt like laughing but she had known somehow that Max would respond this way. He was so wacky. He was probably the only person in the entire Bio Union who would be ecstatic to learn he was not a complete Genhant.

"Guess this is the closest you can come to not being one of those pasted-up concoctions of hopes and dreams you were complaining about."

"Gee, no. I mean I could actually be a total failure . . . a thug . . . maybe a genius, that's the most boring actually, but the possibilities are endless . . . Darci, I could be a criminal!"

"No, *I'm* the criminal, if you'll recall."

"Oh gee, I didn't mean to make fun of your situation. What are your parents saying or doing?"

"What can they do or say? Not much. My dad's ulcer's acting up. My mom's biting her fingernails down to the quick. They're mumbling about going to the Federation Lands in the Western Territory."

Max was quiet now for a long time. "Darci," he finally said.

"Yeah?"

"I just had this really strange thought."

"Nothing strikes me as strange these days," she replied. "But try me anyhow."

"Well, you know how you're . . . well, you've always been interested in words."

"Yeah. It stands to reason. My great-grandfather was a renowned language scientist."

"I know, but mine wasn't, and I'm interested in words too. That's why I like hanging out at the Library of Dead Language, and every once in a while it's like—I can't explain it, but it's as if there are these little rips— tears in my brain."

Darci stopped drinking her liquid sundae and grew still. She sensed that what Max was about to say was very crucial. "Tears in the brain," he repeated. "I mean they aren't bad. It's not like they hurt, but it's almost like . . ."

"Old words come through." Darci finished the sentence for him.

Max nodded. "Do you think that maybe this is special for people like us—masked chimeras? Do you think that because we have some of this very old genetic material something very ancient is trying to push through?"

"It's almost as if we have the memory of the species from before the Reformation."

"Yeah," Max said. "It's like these fossil words aren't

exactly fossils for us. They kind of beat around in some very old part of our brain."

"I think," Darci said slowly, "maybe they want to get out. Maybe they want to be hooked up with meaning again." Darci thought back to that summer evening just a few short weeks before when the Milky Way galaxy quivered in the bucket, when she had looked up at the sky to peer at it as an astronomer in search of old stars but instead had reached out in her mind for another time, an ancient time, a time she thought of as being full of wonder and grace, a time when meaning held fast and did not slip through one's fingers like water.

Max spoke quietly. "You know how they discovered this summer that umbellation was first called cloning in the very earliest days of the Reformation?"

"Yeah," Darci replied.

"Well, guess what?"

"What?"

"They think they are hot on the track of the source meaning of the word 'umbellation'. It has something to do with flowers, clusters of flower petals. Umbellating is like the spreading or something of these flower clusters."

"Figures," Darci said dully.

"What do you mean, 'figures'?"

"It's all part of a lie, a very big lie. It probably began in that time they called the Dark Time. I mean, flowers—who can object to flowers? If you want to do something that is kind of weird or risky, call it a nice, sweet name. Something that has very little to do with what is really happening. It's like there is this separation between the truth of the thing and the words used to describe it. It just widens and widens over time and then the real meaning falls away into this bottomless pit."

"And we're left with the lies."

"The lies and a lot of dead words."

Max stood up. "Come on, we should be going." Slowly Darci turned her head, keeping her eyes low, but watching all the same. There was a comfort here in this quiet place, this soundless, wordless place with just the clink of dishes and cups and the shadows of fingers dancing on the walls.

Max went home with Darci for dinner. Darci hoped it would help perk up the family, for the meals had become long, silent affairs of late, heavy with the weight of 'the problem,' 'the situation,' or once she heard her mother call it, in a low guttural voice to her father, 'the crisis.' They had not told Darci's grandparents. They didn't want to say anything until they knew what they were doing. Darci did not ask her parents much but she sensed that they had discussed 'the situation' with someone else in the underground. They had gotten into the habit of going to bed early. But Darci knew that like herself, her parents lay awake most nights until just before the dawn.

That night, however, after Max left, Darci lay awake thinking about those little rips in the brain that let in echoes of old words, and the shadows of their meanings. She wrestled once more in her thoughts with the word *Original*. She seemed so close to some brink, some horizon of meaning that had previously eluded her when the strong beams of the multiple high-powered searchlights raked through her bedroom window and across the walls and ceiling. In the first glare of the crisscrossing beams, the meaning suddenly exploded in her brain. She felt caught, as if in the first billionth of a second of the event that began the universe—*Original* meant ancient! It meant first! It meant earliest and never before. That was what the word *Original* meant. It was the Beginning!

Then everything happened at once. There was the pounding of feet on the staircase. She was being torn from her bed. There had been no noise until the searchlights. They had come in the darkest part of the night. Even their dogs were quiet. But now there was noise— barks of dogs, sharp commands, the clank of metal. They cuffed her and her parents, shoving them roughly down the stairs. An officer began reading them the Third Degree Highest Order Violation of the Umbellation Statutes. There was a lab technician already jabbing needles into their arms to draw blood, which would provide the incontrovertible evidence that Vivian was an umbula.

She felt a second needle in her arm. Someone was slapping her stomach down on a gurney and pulling up the back of her nightshirt. A sharp sting in the small of her back at the base of her spine. What in the name of Otherness, in the name of God, of the Lord, oh! what sweet names would they patch together to call this— what were they now doing to her family? After all, as the director of the Museum of Reproductive Reformation had told them, the Bio Union was a democracy; in fact this Union was the highest form of civilization. There was choice! The Bio Union was the Cradle of Genetic Democracy. Cradle, Darci thought as they jabbed another needle into her, and she saw her mother crumple to the floor.

Chapter 24

THE MURLOWES WERE TAKEN TO THE highest security prison, which was located a few miles outside the capital city. They were put into separate cells. There were not bars as Darci had always imagined but rather solid steel walls. The door had an eight-inch square, heavy-gauge metal screen through which she could talk to her lawyer. They were all given a lawyer. The window could also be opened from the opposite side to push through small plates of food.

As far as Darci was concerned the lawyer came mostly to get them used to the idea that their situation was hopeless. None of them was allowed any visitors or any communication between themselves. And that of course was what Darci craved most. How were her parents doing? How was Vivian doing? For she had been arrested the same night and brought to the prison the next day. It was on the front page of every newspaper. Darci was surprised that they had been allowed newspapers. There were photographs of herself and Vivian. There were, of course, her old school pictures and family pictures, but Darci realized that GENPOL must have suspected them for several weeks before the arrest, for there was a photo of her with her hair dyed and cropped short. They must have been tracking her and Vivian. Someone in Palmyra must have tipped them off. A darkness welled in Darci as she realized that most likely it had been a climber who had seen them both on the rocks, possibly even someone from camp. She hated to think that the world of rocks and climbing, which she had loved so much, had in fact betrayed her. In reading the newspaper articles she found it slightly odd that no one had linked this umbellation to the underground movement that her parents had told her about.

The buzzer outside her cell rang. It was the lawyer for his daily visit. Darci got up from the cot and went to the screen.

He cleared his throat nervously. "Uh . . ." The sound fell through the mesh like a clod of dirt. "Uh . . ." he said again. Usually he spoke in a rapid-fire nervous style. Darci couldn't blame him for being nervous. The situation was so hopeless and yet for some reason he came, or perhaps was required to come, to the prison each day. Finally he seemed to recover his voice. "Well, Darci, I have some bad news."

Darci wondered what could be worse than her present predicament. But she learned in the next twenty seconds. "Your incineration is scheduled for tomorrow."

"Tomorrow! But that's so soon . . . Has there been a trial?"

"Remember, no regular trials in cases like these. They have all the proof they need."

"What time?"

"Ten o'clock in the morning."

Darci could see the clock in the corridor through the screened window. It was 11:00 now. She had twenty-three hours to live. "Will my parents . . . will they . . ." She hesitated. Language escaped her but why not? Why in this foul world should there be things such as words?

"Yes. Your parents and Vivian too. You'll all go at once."

Then in the hardest act so far of her life Darci said the next words with great dignity and complete clarity. "You mean we shall all be burned alive together."

She heard the sharp intake of breath on the opposite side of the window. "Yes." The word came out strangled. The lawyer turned away and hurried down the corridor.

Darci went back and sat on her cot. How should she spend the last twenty-three hours of her life? What should she do? Say? How should she prepare herself? The Otherness, would the Otherness help her? "Oh, Lord," she finally murmured. The word felt soft on her lips. Perhaps she liked this word rather than the Otherness. "Oh, Lord, oh Lord!" she kept saying and then sometimes she would whisper the word "God."

Darci did not know how many minutes or even hours of these final twenty-three had passed but there was another ring of the buzzer. She got up. This time it was the matron.

She passed the small plate through. It was different food. Before it had been gray meat and applesauce and mushy peas all slopped together. Now it was two pink slices of tenderloin of beef, mashed potatoes squirted decoratively out of a pastry tube, a sprig of parsley as a garnish on top, cranberries, and a frosted cookie. Darci was appalled.

"Your last meal. They try to make it pretty—very good meat, high quality," the matron said.

"Why?" Darci was stunned. "Why?" was all she could say. The totality of the lie was all she could think. Complete and garnished with a little sprig of parsley! She let the plate drop on the floor and began to laugh hysterically. She vaguely remembered hearing an expulsion of air from a jet high up in the corner of her cell, and an odd odor. Her eyes stung slightly and she soon felt very sleepy.

The next thing Darci knew was that it was morning. She heard the clanking of the door to her cell. "Okay, time to get up. I know you feel groggy." Two matrons were shaking her. They were putting her into a kind of jumpsuit. "This will make it go faster, sweetie," they said as they buttoned her into it. "They call this material 'quick flame.' It'll all be over in a very few seconds once they put you in." The words beat dully on her brain. She didn't seem to care.

The matrons were talking between themselves. "She's still pretty groggy."

"Very little muscle response," the other matron said as she stuffed Darci's arms into the sleeves.

"Well, it's better this way. Those airborne sedatives work differently on people. But I noticed the umbula, she was just as groggy."

"Figures."

What Darci would remember would be the grayness. The grayness of everything. From the time she was shaken awake to a kind of mental gray fog in the steel cell to when she was escorted to the armored truck, waiting in the gray half-light of the huge prison garage. They were to be taken to the Incinerarium in four separate vehicles. In the last hour of life they would not even be allowed to ride together. When she stepped out of the vehicle escorted by four GENPOL officers there was no sun. Just a light gray drizzle and thick cloud cover.

They led her to an immense inner courtyard of the Incinerarium. It was filled with thousands of people. There were television cameras and reporters. There was complete silence in the courtyard as Darci was led to a scaffolding in front of the two tall steel doors. In the armored truck on the way to the Incinerarium a GENPOL agent with a very gentle soothing voice had explained precisely what would happen: the two doors that opened to the chute, the electric prods—"Don't worry," he had said, "there won't be that terrible moment when you think I can't do this. The electric prod will send just enough of a shock through you to propel you right into the chute. You won't have time to think. It's a blessing."

He had then explained how they would go in twos. Darci and Vivian first. He didn't explain why but Darci knew. This would be the ultimate punishment for the parents: to see their creations burn.

"Will the Prima be there?" Darci asked.

"We're not sure," the agent replied. "Her implantation just took place a few days ago. It's a delicate time for her. Although we understand she wants to be here. She feels it is an important lesson for the Bio Union."

"Oh." The word was barely audible.

As Darci mounted the platform she saw her parents and Vivian for the first time. Darci understood now that all of them had been given a powerful sedative. There was barely a flicker of recognition in their faces. They seemed as glazed just as she herself felt. She saw her mother look first at Vivian and then at Darci, curiously detached and somewhat confused. Their hands were manacled and they were all dressed in the identical yellow quick-flame jumpsuits.

There was a blast of horns and martial music.

"Citizens, the Prima of the Bio Union."

The Prima, followed by the Prima Matri, appeared from behind a curtain. They were dressed similarly in stylish yellow suits. Darci wondered if the choice of color was somehow a sympathy statement for the victims.

Everyone now rose. Darci felt the hand of a GEN-POL agent put pressure on her elbow to make her stand up. She thought she felt the heat from the Incinerarium. The GENPOL agent had explained that the furnaces had been firing all night and that when they opened the door there would be a great outward rush of heat that could be felt throughout the entire courtyard. A vivid reminder, a conditioning to the law of the land lest any one ever forget and dare dream of committing such a heinous crime.

The people now seated themselves except for Darci,

Vivian, and Darci's parents. They were escorted to stand in front of the great doors. They were lined up two by two. Darci looked at Vivian and smiled ever so slightly. She could not help but think of the fragment she had read from Project Noah. Here they were—two by two, except this was like the reverse, the inside-out version of the story. They were not getting on a boat in order to save the species. They were instead going to be pushed into fire to destroy—what? Suddenly the full irony of this inside-out story struck Darci. They were being destroyed as creatures that man had created and not God. She wanted to turn to Vivian and tell her this story, the Original Story, about man and beast and creeping things, and fowl of the air . . .

An immense silence, however, seemed to engulf Darci. All was still, even as the doors of the Incinerarium opened and a fierce wall of heat rushed out. There was such silence. Thick, immutable silence. She and Vivian faced each other. It was as if silvery filaments of their minds were directly connected. A single star was formed for one brief instant and with it came a single word: "quiescent." This is the quiescence—the starving before the change. Suddenly there was a flash of silver and gold and bright yellow. Then a terrible gasp. "The Prima!" someone screeched. The doors to the Incinerarium swung shut. The heat vanished. Thousands of people remained silent and stunned. Darci and Vivian looked at each another, then turned and looked at the doors. Vivian took Darci's hand. Tears were streaming down her face. "Lana and Stella."

"Who?" said Darci.

"The Prima and the Prima Matri"—her voice caught—"died for us."

"What?" Darci said again.

"The Prima said that the Bio Union must end, so this is how she has ended it."

There was a keening sound of grief as people began to realize what had happened. Some of the people seemed almost frozen. Others stared vacantly into space, their arms and legs quivering almost uncontrollably. Several of the GENPOL officers seemed to be attempting to speak but no sound came from their lips. Then through the keening, the air above thumped with the staccato beat of helicopters.

Darci thought she heard someone say "Bio Rads." Two helicopters landed on the roof spanning the distance between the inner courtyard and the outer walls of the buildings. The courtyard gates swung open. Throughout it all the eerie silence remained. Darci remembered thinking it was truly quiescent. It was as if everything was in a suspended state. Not one GENPOL officer moved against the rebels. The last thing she remembered was being put into a helicopter with her parents and Vivian. She remembered that the man sitting next to the pilot looked familiar. Of course—he had worked with Max's brother at the Library of Dead Language. He was weeping.

Vivian leaned forward and touched the man's arm. "Lana and Stella, they are gone forever, aren't they?"

The man looked at both Darci and Vivian. He nodded, then spoke. "I remember a fragment I was working on. We got some of it back—except possibly for the pronouns. It said we must 'take them and cut them out in little stars, and they will make the face of heaven so fine that all the world will be in love with the night, and pay no worship to the garish sun.' That fragment reminds me of Stella and Lana."

For Darci, every word sang with meaning and with mystery. "Who wrote that?" she asked.

"We think it's the writer that might have been called the Bard by the Ancients."

In the gathering light of the morning the helicopter flew over the Kerals for the last time and disappeared into the night.

.

Chapter 25

Nine months later, New Eden, a settlement in the Western Territory of the Federation Lands

THE LABOR BEGAN SHORTLY AFTER midnight. Darci and Vivian and Max had stayed up all night outside the cabin while Juditha and several other women tended a woman named Johanna. Vivian's uncle Walter came outside when he could be spared to give an update. The night had begun to thin into the first grayness of the dawn and the sky down near the horizon began to warm with a tinge of pink. Darci thought back on the last several months. It was while they were in the helicopter that the man who had worked at the library told them that the implantation had never taken place, or at least not in the manner that the citizens of the Bio Union had believed. When Lana and Stella had realized that the Primarchy must end, they knew that any embryo bearing their genetic material had to be sent far away if they wanted it to live anything resembling a normal life. There was only one safe way to accomplish this, which was to implant the embryo in another woman. Lana had convinced Walter of this without revealing to him that it was very possible that she and Stella might have to die to achieve their goals. Thus Walter had agreed to the implantation in Johanna, who had been the Prima's personal maid.

Walter came out now. There would always be a lingering sadness in Walter's eyes. It reminded Darci of the morning mist that gathered in a meadow beyond the cabin, but now at least there were traces of a weak light. Darci, Vivian, and Max looked up. "Well?" said Darci.

"Should be very soon. But one never knows. You know this is a first for all of us. No hospital. And . . ." He hesitated.

"And what?" Vivian asked. "Is there something you're not telling us, Uncle Walter?"

Walter's eyes actually twinkled. "I want it to be a surprise."

"No, no surprises," Vivian said emphatically.

"This will be a good surprise, believe me!" He disappeared inside.

Darci didn't quite understand what the surprise could

be. The baby was a masked chimera. It would have traits of Lana and Walter. Blue eyes, maybe green like Lana's, but like all babies just that deep no-color gray at first. Blonde hair, maybe black. Maybe a combination. What other surprises could there be?

Suddenly they heard it. A wet loud howl that pealed through the dawn. They were immediately on their feet. Another woman came out and motioned them inside.

They crowded into the small bedroom. Johanna lay back, exhausted, against the pillows. Walter held a tiny bundle in his arms.

"Can we see? Can we see?" Vivian whispered.

"Of course," her uncle Walter said. "Sit down, Vivian. Hold your new cousin."

Vivian sat down and Walter placed the tiny bundle in her arms. Max and Darci crowded around. The little red face looked wizened and old as time, but when the eyes opened and the three children peered into them it was as if they were seeing glints of a dark and shining new universe. The baby grew quiet and seemed to focus on the young faces. "What's her name?" Darci asked softly.

"Alan," Walter replied, smiling.

"But Alan's a boy's name, Uncle Walter," Vivian said, still looking at the baby.

"But this is a little boy and his name is Alan."

A New Day

THEY CLIMBED THROUGH SHAFTS of rosy light in the rugged red rock country of the Western Territories. They had started from the base at dawn when the light was cool and lavender. The best part of climbing out here, Darci thought, was the way in which the light changed the color of the rock. It was as if you were climbing though a rainbow. Darci was climbing lead on a flake that separated from the main rock face of a formation called the Horseteeth. Vivian was below belaying her, ready to lock off if she fell.

Vivian now looked up at Darci, who was some fifty feet higher. She had reached the central crack of the flake. This was their favorite part of the route. At the top of the crack there was a corner that required wide stemming action. In the beginning of the summer neither Darci nor Vivian could do it. But now they had both stretched the ligaments of their upper legs so they had actually increased their range of motion and they could easily straddle this corner. Then it was only fifteen feet to the top. They had topped three times now. Today was to be their fourth.

Darci was at the stemming point. She swung her leg straight out at a ninety-degree angle to her body. She was around the corner within seconds. And then in another five minutes, at the top.

"I'm here," she called down to Vivian.

"I'm coming," Vivian called back

The top of the flake was no larger than a good-size dining table but you could see the entire territory unfolding beneath you. The red rock country bristled like a brush with its needlelike spires. At the farthest edges the spires smudged into a smoky blue mist. That was where the River of Winds formations began. Darci squinted. She and Vivian would climb them some day. Walter said he would take them there. She looked down now. She could hear Vivian's breathing as she made her way up the last feet of the crack. Darci saw the long tanned leg wing out in the stem move to wrap around the corner. She blinked. Vivian was doing it differently. Her leg was hiked up much higher. It was at nearly a forty-five-degree angle to her body. The breath locked in Darci throat. This seemed like a risky move. How had she ever thought of it? How could her leg swing that high when she was in that position? But she was around the corner in a blink.

"Hi." Darci saw her own face grinning up at her.

"How'd you do that?" Darci asked

"I'm not sure. It just sort of came to me in a flash. There's a good heel hold up there if your leg can make it."

They both looked at each other and smiled. They knew the answer. Both their legs could make it, but only one of them had thought of it. They sat with their feet dangling over the edge, the sun on their faces. Vast stretches of rose and gold light spread out across the world. They had climbed to the top of the rainbow and into a new day.

Afterword

A Comfortable Distance?

When I first read *Brave New World* by Aldous Huxley as a teenager in the 1960s, I, like so many who had read this classic, was appalled and frightened by the surrealistic scientific world it presented. As horrified as I was I never seriously thought anything approaching that world, especially that of mechanized human reproduction and genetic engineering, would ever happen within my lifetime.

Part of being a teenager, at least back then, was a hypersensitivity to the here and now with a somewhat casual belief in the future. But even parents and teachers, responsible adults charged with our upbringing, with paying mortgages and saving for college educations, would have been hard-pressed to believe what would happen in the next decade, let alone three decades, in terms of genetic engineering. The Brave New World would begin to happen long before the close of the millennium. I was right to be horrified. I was wrong to think that I could enjoy my horror in a purely literary sense at a comfortable distance.

The first time I ever heard the word *clone* or *cloning* was in a college biology class. At that time the word was not used in reference to humans at all but only for plants and microbes. Perhaps if I had taken an advanced biology course—but I would not, for I was a firmly entrenched English major and a real science-phobe—I might have heard about the attempts of a British embryologist named John Gurdon to clone an animal—a frog in this case. But the word *cloning* had not at all become a part of the popular culture or the public vocabulary.

In the late 1970s the first instance that I can recall of a reference to cloning in terms of popular culture was in the Woody Allen film *Sleeper*, in which a futuristic society had somehow preserved the nose of their dead dictator and were trying to bring him back through cloning. It was a sidesplittingly funny movie, and what better way to keep things at a comfortable distance than through outrageous humor.

Then in the 1980s we began to hear about the Harvard Mouse, or the transgenic mouse embryo into which foreign DNA had been introduced and successfully incorporated into one of its chromosomes. This of course anticipated marvelous things, for it meant that scientists could gain deeper insight into how human cancer cells grew and spread. The little mouse would be a kind of living crystal ball for cancer researchers. It also meant that the genetic engineering of human embryos was no longer a figment of a science-fiction writer's fevered imagination. The fiction within a few short years had turned into fact. If scientists could manipulate the embryo of a mouse to carry a specific human gene they could do the same with humans and introduce desirable genes into human embryos.

For the next decade it seemed we were reading about amazing advances in the realm of genetic engineering every month. Many of us remember the joy with which the world greeted Louise Brown, the first in vitro, or "test tube" baby, in which the egg was fertilized in a petri dish. Now there are thousands of in vitro babies and Louise is college age.

Technologies were available to me as an expectant mother that were not available to my own mother or my older sister. Amniocentesis could be performed at the sixteenth week of pregnancy to screen for a variety of genetic diseases. We could choose to end pregnancies if our child was doomed to a disastrous life of reduced intelligence or some painful chronic illness. When my own children were born my first question always was "Is IT all right?" By "all right" I meant did the baby have all its fingers, toes, arms, legs? Was it perfectly healthy? I didn't care about the sex, but I wanted a perfect baby. Perfect to me meant healthy and smart; maybe not beautiful but presentable.

In the early nineties we felt a bit nauseous when we saw the newspaper picture of that little mouse with the ear growing from its back. Why would scientists do something like that? What possible result could this yield? Was it a straight course to the cure for cancer? Well, maybe if that was the reason, we nonscientists out there could tolerate it. But shades of Dr. Frankenstein were creeping across our imaginations.

Then in February 1997 our imaginations were profoundly stirred with the announcement of Dolly, the sheep in Scotland that had been cloned from not just an embryonic cell, but a full-fledged adult sheep cell. How had they reprogrammed that adult cell to make a clone in baby form? Dolly seemed to break through all the technical barriers in cloning. It was hailed around the world as an astonishing accomplishment. But that comfortable distance was closing in fast upon us.

The only stretch I have made in writing this book is indeed a chronological one of millennia. I have set this book, ironically, at a comfortable distance within the fourth millennia. Indeed this is an artistic distance I felt necessary to write the story. However, *all* of which I write has begun to happen. Every single genetic engineering strategy that I mention in this book is based upon one that has already been executed or is in a developmental stage right now in the year 1998. For example chimeras were actually conceived and executed over thirty years ago. The word "chimera" refers to a fire-breathing monster from Greek mythology with a lion's head, a goat's trunk, and a dragon's hindquarters. But the myth came to life in the early 1960s in a decidedly less monstrous and fiery incarnation as a mouse in which two embryos were combined into one and whose cells derived from two pairs of parent mice. Such a creation is known as a chimeric mouse. It looks and behaves like a perfectly normal mouse.

The idea of it happening with a mouse is perhaps tolerable but people might indeed become nervous if they thought of combining two human embryos, or for that matter teasing apart embryonic material in the manner I have suggested in reference to the "embryokins" in *Star Split*. However, such chimeras have already occurred naturally in humans. Since the research on chimeras was begun geneticists have in rare instances identified natural-born chimeras in humans. Such human chimeras, although not involving two sets of parents, were the result of two embryos fusing after two eggs had been released during ovulation and fertilized. It is rare but it has happened and with genetic engineering it would be not all that difficult to replicate it on demand and with two sets of parents if desired.

The creation of Dolly was an accomplishment that began to worry the public in a way no other scientific advance in the realm of reproductive genetics ever had. It was indeed a clear signal that Huxley's world was here and that controls were needed. There was no longer a comfortable distance. That very week Congress began debating issues of cloning and genetic engineering. It was no longer a question of when but how such genetic engineering procedures and science might be abused and what would be the consequences. We were now firmly treading in what had always been considered God's territory.

K.L.
December 1998
Cambridge, Massachusets

ACKNOWLEDGMENTS

Many of the ideas and notions that I explore in *Star Split* have been discussed extensively in several excellent nonfiction books and articles. I owe a great debt of gratitude to Gina Kolata, a reporter for *The New York Times*, for her excellent coverage of the cloning of the sheep Dolly, as well as her insightful book *The Road to Dolly and the Path Ahead*; to Lee Silver, a professor at Princeton University in the Department of Molecular Biology, and his wonderful book *Re-Making Eden: Cloning and Beyond in a Brave New World*; Steven Levy, author of *Artificial Life: The Quest for a New Creation*; John Robertson's book *Children of Choice: Freedom and the New Reproductive Technologies*.

There are other men and women who are scientists and theologians too numerous to mention who continue to grapple with the moral and ethical implications of these new technologies. I am in awe of their tenacity, their insight, and their courage not to accept easy answers to these questions that ultimately define the meaning of life and the meaning of being human.